Rex Stout

REX STOUT, the creator of Nero Wolfe, was born in Noblesville, Indiana, in 1886, the sixth of nine children of John and Lucetta Todhunter Stout, both Quakers. Shortly after his birth the family moved to Wakarusa, Kansas. He was educated in a country school, but by the age of nine he was recognized throughout the state as a prodigy in arithmetic. Mr. Stout briefly attended the University of Kansas, but he left to enlist in the Navy and spent the next two years as a warrant officer on board President Theodore Roosevelt's yacht. When he left the Navy in 1908, Rex Stout began to write freelance articles and worked as a sightseeing guide and an itinerant book-keeper. Later he devised and implemented a school banking system which was installed in four hundred cities and towns throughout the country. In 1927 Mr. Stout retired from the world of finance and, with the proceeds of his banking scheme, left for Paris to write serious fiction. He wrote three novels that received favorable reviews before turning to detective fiction. His first Nero Wolfe novel, *Fer-de-Lance*, appeared in 1934. It was followed by many others, among them, *Too Many Cooks*, *The Silent Speaker*, *If Death Ever Slept*, *The Doorbell Rang*, and *Please Pass the Guilt*, which established Nero Wolfe as a leading character on a par with Erle Stanley Gardner's famous protagonist, Perry Mason. During World War II Rex Stout waged a personal campaign against Nazism as chairman of the War Writers' Board, master of ceremonies of the radio program "Speaking of Liberty," and member of several national committees. After the war he turned his attention to mobilizing public opinion against the wartime use of thermonuclear devices, was an active leader in the Authors' Guild, and resumed writing his Nero Wolfe novels. Rex Stout died in 1975 at the age of eighty-eight. A month before his death he published his seventy-second Nero Wolfe mystery, *A Family Affair*. Ten years later, a seventy-third Nero Wolfe mystery was discovered and published in *Death Times Three*

The Rex Stout Library

REX STOUT

Plot It Yourself

*Introduction
by Susan Dunlap*

BANTAM BOOKS

NEW YORK · TORONTO · LONDON · SYDNEY · AUCKLAND

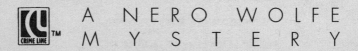

A NERO WOLFE
MYSTERY

PLOT IT YOURSELF
A Bantam Crime Line Book / published by arrangement
with Viking Penguin

PUBLISHING HISTORY
Bantam reissue edition / July 1994
Viking edition published October 1959
Mystery Guild edition published February 1960
Bantam edition published December 1960

CRIME LINE and the portrayal of a boxed "cl" are trademarks of Bantam
Books, a division of Bantam Doubleday Dell Publishing Group, Inc.

ISBN 0-553-25363-8

Published simultaneously in the United States and Canada

Bantam Books are published by Bantam Books, a division of Bantam Doubleday Dell Publishing Group, Inc. Its trademark, consisting of the words "Bantam
Books" and the portrayal of a rooster, is Registered in U.S. Patent and Trademark Office and in other countries. Marca Registrada. Bantam Books, 1540
Broadway, New York, New York 10036.

Introduction

While finishing a manuscript, I'm frantically rethinking sentences, nervously pondering tempo, adding description, clarifying things that seemed quite clear in the previous draft, again reconsidering tempo. At the same time, I'm trying to keep in mind all the motives of all my suspects, the clues and where I've mentioned them, and the red herrings I've sprinkled throughout four hundred pages. I feel like one of those performers on an old TV variety show, racing up and down the line of a dozen plates spinning on edge, keeping them all rotating at once.

Then I think to myself (with only a soupçon of self-pity): There has to be an easier way to write a book.

And so Rex Stout must have thought as he concocted *Plot It Yourself*.

Stout, of course, was a master. There *is* an easier way, he concluded: Steal someone else's plot, with the descriptions done, the clues in place, and the herrings swimming among them. And while you're at it, why take unnecessary chances? Lift that plot from a best-seller! And easier yet, don't even bother to type out all four hundred pages. Just make an outline, swear you'd sent it to the author several years earlier with a request for a critique, and insist that, instead of critiquing it, the greedy writer plagiarized it. Yes, indeed, Mr. Stout must have thought, every year that would save months of worry and grumbling, and carton upon carton of crashing china. I can imagine the grin on Rex Stout's face as he created the characters to operate this scheme.

And that grin spreads to us readers as we see the puzzle it presents Nero Wolfe in *Plot It Yourself*.

In Rex Stout's work the puzzle is paramount. It is the puzzle that intrigues the great Nero Wolfe; the more baffling the case, the greater the challenge. It's no problem for Wolfe to keep a dozen plates spinning. He could keep a hundred spinning (as long as he didn't have to leave his armchair to do it). And his creator, speaking through Archie Goodwin, keeps us alert to the import of each new plate as it starts to rotate and every question it tosses off with the discovery of every clue.

Because Stout does speak through Archie Goodwin, we see the import of the clues that a brighter-than-average person would get, but not the ones that are clear only to a genius like Wolfe. We watch with amazement, and we delight as the genius deciphers it all.

All the while we have the pleasure of looking through the eyes of a guy we accept as a snappy, think-on-your-feet representative of ourselves, and we have a chuckle at Wolfe's oddities: his seventh-of-a-ton size, his unbreakable rules (no talking business at meals, no interruption of orchid-care hours, and never *never* leave the house on business). Of course, no rule is absolute, and when Wolfe is forced to break each one, that just heightens the tension.

But it is these very rules that make Nero Wolfe

such an appealing character. Who among us would not like to be a curmudgeon so superior (in fact, almost as superior as he assumes) that the rest of humanity is forced to accept his terms? The impatient cool their heels till Wolfe has misted the last orchid, the clock has struck eleven, and he is willing to descend to his office. Pompous bigshots must sit tight and listen. And when the police arrive at the door, he doesn't always open it.

Yet Wolfe is endearing. Cutting as he is with the self-important, he can be sensitive with the unsure. As for himself, no one is a harsher critic of his oversights. And very occasionally—oh, so humiliatingly—he must admit he has been taken in.

And then Archie Goodwin—and we—can snicker silently.

Much as we enjoy identifying with Wolfe's power, we are happier looking at him through Archie's eyes. Many of us mystery readers are brats at heart. We cheer the Davids as they aim their stones at life's Goliaths, we love Calvin of "Calvin and Hobbes" when he baits his mother, father, teacher, or any other authority. We are the little kids sitting in the back of the room ready with spitballs in hand or, more likely, smart remarks to whisper to a neighbor. We love Archie Goodwin as he makes snide comments about Wolfe's counting his beer-bottle caps; we're delighted when Goodwin finds the truth inadequate and fabricates on-the-spot explanations, rationales, or invitations too intriguing to be refused. We worry when he chances being caught red-handed in the midst of breaking and entering.

But it's not only Wolfe and Goodwin that draw us to the Stout books. It's the setting. The brownstone we'd all kill for. Wolfe's office with its yellow chairs for clients, suspects, and witnesses, and the red chair for the most favored of them. Manhattan, where life strides strong at all hours. The era of the stories varies from 1934 to 1975, but there is always the feel of the thirties and forties, the days of black-and-white movies, when things were slick, and smart, and possible. When New York was the center of the universe. When life was fast, good and evil were crisp, and patter was breezy.

The Nero Wolfe books could be classified as Manhattan Cozies. The murders, by and large, happen offstage. Rarely do we care enough about the deceased to mourn his passing. *Au contraire*, we're delighted that his sacrifice has given us another clue, or further confusion. We don't want to slip into the mire of care. When those plates start to spin, we don't want to think about the danger of shards of china; we want to sit back and enjoy the spectacle.

And Rex Stout gives us the best spin in town.

Susan Dunlap

Plot It Yourself

Chapter 1

I divide the books Nero Wolfe reads into four grades: A, B, C, and D. If, when he comes down to the office from the plant rooms at six o'clock, he picks up his current book and opens to his place before he rings for beer, and if his place was marked with a thin strip of gold, five inches long and an inch wide, which was presented to him some years ago by a grateful client, the book is an A. If he picks up the book before he rings, but his place was marked with a piece of paper, it is a B. If he rings and then picks up the book, and he had dog-eared a page to mark his place, it is a C. If he waits until Fritz has brought the beer and he has poured to pick up the book, and his place was dog-eared, it's a D. I haven't kept score, but I would say that of the two hundred or so books he reads in a year not more than five or six get an A.

At six o'clock that Monday afternoon in May I was at my desk, checking the itemization of expenses that was to accompany the bill going to the Spooner Corporation for a job we had just finished, when the sound came of his elevator jolting to a stop and his footsteps in the hall. He entered, crossed to the oversized made-to-order chair behind his desk, sat, picked up *Why the Gods Laugh,* by Philip Harvey, opened to the page marked with the strip of gold, read a paragraph, and reached to the button at the edge of his desk without taking his eyes from the page. As he did so, the phone rang.

I got it. "Nero Wolfe's residence, Archie Goodwin speaking." Up to six o'clock I say "Nero Wolfe's office." After six I say "residence."

A tired baritone said, "I'd like to speak to Mr. Wolfe. This is Philip Harvey."

"He'll want to know what about. If you please?"

"I'll tell him. I'm a writer. I'm acting on behalf of the National Association of Authors and Dramatists."

"Did you write a book called *Why the Gods Laugh?*"

"I did."

"Hold the wire." I covered the transmitter and turned. "If that book has any weak spots here's your chance. The guy who wrote it wants to speak to you."

He looked up. "Philip Harvey?"

"Right."

"What does he want?"

"He says he'll tell you. Probably to ask you what page you're on."

He closed the book on a finger to keep his place and took his phone. "Yes, Mr. Harvey?"

"Is this Nero Wolfe?"

"Yes."

"You may possibly have heard my name."

"Yes."

"I want to make an appointment to consult you. I am chairman of the Joint Committee on Plagiarism of the National Association of Authors and Dramatists

and the Book Publishers of America. How about tomorrow morning?"

"I know nothing about plagiarism, Mr. Harvey."

"We'll tell you about it. We have a problem we
want you to handle. There'll be six or seven of us,
members of the committee. How about tomorrow
morning?"

"I'm not a lawyer. I'm a detective."

"I know you are. How about ten o'clock?"

Of course that wouldn't do, since it would take
more than an author, even of a book that rated an A, to
break into Wolfe's two morning hours with the orchids,
from nine to eleven. Harvey finally settled for a quarter past eleven. When we hung up I asked Wolfe if I
should check, and he nodded and went back to his
book. I rang Lon Cohen at the *Gazette* and learned
that the National Association of Authors and Dramatists was it. All the dramatists anyone had ever heard
of were members, and most of the authors, the chief
exceptions being some scattered specimens who hadn't
decided if they cared to associate with the human race
—or had decided that they didn't. The Book Publishers of America was also it, a national organization of
all the major firms and many of the minor ones. I
passed the information along to Wolfe, but I wasn't
sure he listened. He was reading.

That evening around midnight, when I got home
after taking a friend to a show, *A Barrel of Love*, by
Mortimer Oshin, Wolfe had just finished his book
and was making room for it on one of the shelves over
by the big globe. As I tried the door of the safe I
spoke.

"Why not leave it on your desk?"

He grunted. "Mr. Harvey's self-esteem needs no

sop. If he were not so skillful a writer he would be insufferable. Why curry him?"

Before I went up two flights to my room I looked up "curry" in the dictionary. Check. I won't live long enough to see the day when Wolfe curries anybody including me.

Chapter 2

At 11:20 the next morning, Tuesday, Wolfe, seated at his desk, sent his eyes from left to right and back again, rested them on Philip Harvey, and inquired, "You're the spokesman, Mr. Harvey?"

Since Harvey had made the appointment and was chairman of the committee, I had put him in the red leather chair near the end of Wolfe's desk. He was a middle-aged shorty with a round face, round shoulders, and a round belly. The other five were in an arc on yellow chairs that I had had ready for them. Their names, supplied by Harvey, were in my notebook. The one nearest me, the big blond guy in a brown suit with tan stripes, was Gerald Knapp, president of Knapp and Bowen. The one next to him, the wiry-looking bantam with big ears and slick black hair, was Reuben Imhof of the Victory Press. The female about my age who might have been easy to look at if her nose would stop twitching was Amy Wynn. I had seen a couple of reviews of her novel, *Knock at My Door*, but it wasn't on Wolfe's shelves. The tall gray-haired one with a long bony face was Thomas Dexter of Title House. The one at the far end of the arc, with thick lips and deep-set dark eyes, slouching in his chair with his left ankle on his right knee, was Mortimer Oshin. He had written the play, *A Barrel of Love*, which I had seen last evening. He had lit three cigarettes in eight minutes, and with two of the matches he had missed the ashtray on a stand at his elbow and they had landed on the rug.

Philip Harvey cleared his throat. "You'll need all the details," he said, "but first I'll outline it. You said you know nothing about plagiarism, but I assume you know what it is. Of course a charge of plagiarism against a book or a play is dealt with by the author and publisher, or the playwright and producer, but a situation has developed that needs something more than defending individual cases. That's why the NAAD and the BPA have set up this joint committee. I may say that we, the NAAD, appreciate the cooperation of the BPA. In a plagiarism suit it's the author that gets stuck, not the publisher. In all book contracts the author agrees to indemnify the publisher for any liabilities, losses, damages, expenses—"

Reuben Imhof cut in. "Now wait a minute. What is agreed and what actually happens are two different things. Actually, in a majority of cases, the publisher suffers—"

"The suffering publisher!" Amy Wynn cried, her nose twitching. Mortimer Oshin had a comment too, and four of them were speaking at once. I didn't try to sort it out for my notebook.

Wolfe raised his voice. "If you please! You started it, Mr. Harvey. If the interests of author and publisher are in conflict, why a joint committee?"

"Oh, they're not always in conflict." Harvey was smiling, not apologetically. "The interests of slave and master often jibe; they do in this situation. I merely mentioned *en passant* that the author gets stuck. We deeply appreciate the cooperation of the BPA. It's damned generous of them."

"You were going to outline the situation."

"Yes. In the past four years there have been five major charges of plagiarism." Harvey took papers from his pocket, unfolded them, and glanced at the top sheet. "In February nineteen fifty-five, McMurray and Company published *The Color of Passion*, a novel by Ellen Sturdevant. By the middle of April it was at the top of the fiction best-seller list. In June the publishers received a letter from a woman named Alice Porter, claiming that the novel's plot and characters, and all important details of the plot development, with only the setting and names changed, had been stolen from a story written by her, never published, entitled 'There Is Only Love.' She said she had sent the story, twenty-four typewritten pages, to Ellen Sturdevant in November nineteen fifty-two, with a note asking for suggestions for its improvement. It had never been acknowledged or returned. Ellen Sturdevant denied that she had ever seen any such story. One day in August, when she was at her summer home in Vermont, a local woman in her employ came to her with something she said she had found in a bureau drawer. It was twenty-four typewritten sheets, and the top one was headed, 'There Is Only Love, by Alice Porter.' Its plot and characters and many details were the same as those of Ellen Sturdevant's novel, though in much shorter form. The woman, named Billings, admitted that she had been persuaded by Alice Porter to search the house for the typescript—persuaded by the offer of a hundred dollars if she found it. But, having found it, she had a pang of conscience and brought it to her employer. Mrs. Sturdevant has told me that her first impulse was to burn it, but on second thought she realized that that wouldn't do, since Mrs. Billings couldn't be expected to perjure herself on a witness stand, and she phoned her attorney in New York."

Harvey upturned a palm. "That's the meat of it. I may say that I am convinced, and so is everyone who knows her, that Ellen Sturdevant had never seen that typescript before. It was a plant. The case never went to trial. It was settled out of court. Mrs. Sturdevant paid Alice Porter eighty-five thousand dollars."

Wolfe grunted. "There's nothing I could do about it now."

"We know you can't. We don't expect you to. But that's only the beginning." Harvey looked at the second sheet of paper. "In January nineteen fifty-six, Title House published *Hold Fast to All I Give You*, a novel by Richard Echols. Will you tell him about it, Mr. Dexter? Briefly?"

Thomas Dexter passed a hand over his gray hair. "I'll make it as brief as I can," he said. "It's a long story. The publication date was January nineteenth. Within a month we were shipping five thousand a week. By the end of April nine thousand a week. On May sixth we got a letter from a man named Simon Jacobs. It stated that in February nineteen fifty-four he had sent the manuscript of a novelette he had written, entitled 'What's Mine Is Yours,' to the literary agency of Norris and Baum. Norris and Baum had been Echols' agent for years. Jacob enclosed a photostat of a letter he had received from Norris and Baum, dated March twenty-sixth, nineteen fifty-four, returning the manuscript and saying that they couldn't take on any new clients. The letter mentioned the title of the manuscript, 'What's Mine Is Yours.' It was bona fide; there was a copy of it in Norris and Baum's files; but no one there could remember anything about it.

More than two years had passed, and they get a great many unsolicited manuscripts."

Dexter took a breath. "Jacobs claimed that the plot of his novelette was original and unique, also the characters, and that the plot and characters of *Hold Fast to All I Give You*, Echols' novel, were obviously a steal. He said he would be glad to let us inspect his manuscript—that's how he put it—and would give us a copy if we wanted one. His presumption was that someone at Norris and Baum had either told Echols about it or had let him read it. Everyone at Norris and Baum denied it, and so did Echols, and we at Title House believe them. Utterly. But a plagiarism suit is a tricky thing. There is something about the idea of a successful author stealing his material from an unsuccessful author that seems to appeal to ordinary people, and juries are made up of ordinary people. It dragged along for nearly a year. The final decision was left to Echols and his attorney, but we at Title House approved of it. They decided not to risk a trial. Jacobs was paid ninety thousand dollars for a general release. Though we were not obligated by contract, Title House contributed one-fourth of it, twenty-one thousand, five hundred."

"It should have been half," Harvey said, not arguing, just stating a fact.

Wolfe asked, "Did you get a copy of Jacobs' manuscript?"

Dexter nodded. "Certainly. It supported his claim. The plot and characters were practically identical."

"Indeed. Again, Mr. Harvey, it seems to be too late."

"We're getting hotter," Harvey said. "Wait till you hear the rest of it. Next: In November nineteen fifty-six, Nahm and Son published *Sacred or Profane*, a novel by Marjorie Lippin. Like all of her previous books, it had a big sale; the first printing was forty thousand." He consulted his papers. "On March twenty-first, nineteen fifty-seven, Marjorie Lippin died of a heart attack. On April ninth Nahm and Son received a letter from a woman named Jane Ogilvy. Her claim was almost identical with the one Alice Porter had made on *The Color of Passion*—that in June nineteen fifty-five she had sent the manuscript of a twenty-page story, entitled 'On Earth but Not in Heaven,' to Marjorie Lippin, with a letter asking for her opinion of it, that it had never been acknowledged or returned, and that the plot and characters of *Sacred or Profane* had been taken from it. Since Mrs. Lippin was dead she couldn't answer to the charge, and on April fourteenth, only five days after Nahm and Son got the letter, the executor of Mrs. Lippin's estate, an officer of a bank, found the manuscript of the story, as described by Jane Ogilvy, in a trunk in the attic of Mrs. Lippin's home. He considered it his duty to produce it, and he did so. With Mrs. Lippin dead, a successful challenge of the claim seemed hopeless, but her heirs, her son and daughter, were too stubborn to see it, and they wanted to clear her name of the stain. They even had her body exhumed for an autopsy, but it confirmed her death from a natural cause, a heart attack. The case finally went to trial last October, and a jury awarded Jane Ogilvy one hundred and thirty-five thousand dollars. It was paid by the estate. Nahm and Son didn't see fit to contribute."

"Why the hell should they?" Gerald Knapp demanded.

Harvey smiled at him. "The NAAD appreciates your cooperation, Mr. Knapp. I'm merely giving the record."

Dexter told Knapp, "Oh, skip it. It's common knowledge that Phil Harvey has an ulcer. That's why the gods laugh."

Harvey transferred the smile from Knapp and Bowen to Title House. "Many thanks for the plug, Mr. Dexter. At all bookstores—maybe." He returned to Wolfe. "The next one wasn't a novel; it was a play—*A Barrel of Love*, by Mortimer Oshin. You tell it, Mr. Oshin."

The dramatist squashed a cigarette in the tray, his fifth or sixth—I had lost count. "Very painful, this is," he said. He was a tenor. "Nauseous. We opened on Broadway February twenty-fifth last year, and when I say we had a smash hit I'm merely giving the record like Mr. Harvey. Around the middle of May the producer, Al Friend, got a letter from a man named Kenneth Rennert. The mixture as before. It said he had sent me an outline for a play in August nineteen fifty-six, entitled 'A Bushel of Love,' with a letter asking me to collaborate with him on writing it. He demanded a million dollars, which was a compliment. Friend turned the letter over to me, and my lawyer answered it, telling Rennert he was a liar, which he already knew. But my lawyer knew about the three cases you have just heard described, and he had me take precautions. He and I made a thorough search of my apartment on Sixty-fifth Street, every inch of it, and also my house in the country at Silvermine, Connecticut, and I made arrangements that would have made it tough for anybody trying to plant something at either place."

Oshin lit a cigarette and missed the ashtray with the match. "That was wasted effort. As you may know, a playwright must have an agent. I had had one named Jack Sandler that I couldn't get along with, and a month after *A Barrel of Love* opened I had quit him and got another one. One weekend in July, Sandler phoned me in the country and said he had found something in his office and would drive over from his place near Danbury to show it to me. He did. It was a typewritten six-page outline of a play in three acts by Kenneth Rennert, entitled 'A Bushel of Love.' Sandler said it had been found by his secretary when she was cleaning out an old file."

He ditched the cigarette. "As I said, nauseous. Sandler said he would burn it in my presence if I said the word, but I wouldn't trust the bastard. He said he and his secretary would sign affidavits that they had never seen the outline before and it must have been sneaked into the file by somebody, but what the hell, I was somebody. I took it to my lawyer, and he had a talk with Sandler, whom he knew pretty well, and the secretary. He didn't think that either of them had a hand in the plant, and I agreed with him. But also he didn't think we could count on Sandler not to get word to Rennert that the outline had been found, and I agreed with that too. And that's what the bastard did, because in September Rennert brought an action for damages, and he wouldn't have done that if he hadn't known he could get evidence about the outline. A million dollars. My lawyer has entered a countersuit, and I paid a detective agency six thousand dollars in three months trying to get support for it, with no luck. My lawyer thinks we'll have to settle."

"I dislike covering ground that has already been trampled," Wolfe said. "You omitted a detail. The outline resembled your play?"

"It didn't resemble it, it *was* my play, without the dialogue."

Wolfe's eyes went to Harvey. "That makes four. You said five?"

Harvey nodded. "The last one is fresher, but one member of the cast is the same as in the first one. Alice Porter. The woman who got eighty-five thousand dollars out of Ellen Sturdevant. She's coming back for more."

"Indeed."

"Yes. Three months ago the Victory Press published *Knock at My Door*, a novel by Amy Wynn. Amy?"

Amy Wynn's nose twitched. "I'm not very good . . ." She stopped and turned to Imhof, at her left. "You tell it, Reuben."

Imhof gave her shoulder a little pat. "You're plenty good, Amy," he assured her. He focused on Wolfe. "This one is fresh all right. We published Miss Wynn's book on February fourth, and we ordered the sixth printing, twenty thousand, yesterday. That will make the total a hundred and thirty thousand. Ten days ago we received a letter signed Alice Porter, dated May seventh, saying that *Knock at My Door* was taken from an unpublished story she wrote three years ago, with the title 'Opportunity Knocks.' That she sent the story to Amy Wynn in June of nineteen fifty-seven, with a letter asking for comment and criticism, and it has never been acknowledged or returned. According to pattern. Of course we showed the letter to Miss Wynn. She assured us that she had never received any such story or letter, and we accepted her assurance without reservation. Not having a lawyer or an agent, she asked us what she should do. We told her to make sure without delay that no such manuscript was concealed in her home, or any other premises where she could be supposed to have put it, such as the home of a close relative, and to take all possible steps to guard against an attempt to plant the manuscript. Our attorney wrote a brief letter to Alice Porter, rejecting her claim, and upon investigation he learned that she is the Alice Porter who made the claim against Ellen Sturdevant in nineteen fifty-five. I telephoned the executive secretary of the National Association of Authors and Dramatists to suggest that it might be desirable to make Miss Wynn a member of the Joint Committee on Plagiarism, which had been formed only a month previously, and that was done the next day. I was myself already a member. That's how it stands. No further communication has been received from Alice Porter."

Wolfe's eyes moved. "You have taken the steps suggested, Miss Wynn?"

"Of course." She wasn't bad-looking when her nose stayed put. "Mr. Imhof had his secretary help me look. We didn't find it—anything."

"Where do you live?"

"I have a little apartment in the Village—Arbor Street."

"Does anyone live with you?"

"No." She flushed a little, which made her almost pretty. "I have never married."

"How long had you lived there?"

"A little more than a year. I moved there in March last year—fourteen months."

"Where had you lived?"

"On Perry Street. I shared an apartment with two other girls."

"How long had you lived there?"

"About three years." Her nose twitched. "I don't quite see how that matters."

"It might. You were living there in June nineteen fifty-seven, when Alice Porter claims she sent you the story. That would be a suitable place for the story to be found. Did you and Mr. Imhof's secretary search that apartment?"

"No." Her eyes had widened. "Of course. Good heavens! Of course! I'll do it right away."

"But you can't guard against the future." Wolfe wiggled a finger. "I offer a suggestion. Arrange immediately to have that apartment and the one you now occupy searched throughout by two reliable persons, preferably a man and a woman, who have no connection with you or the Victory Press. You should not be present. Tell them that they must be so thorough that when they are through they must be prepared to testify under oath that no such manuscript was on the premises—unless, of course, they find it. If you don't know how to go about getting someone for the job, Mr. Imhof will, or his attorney—or I could. Will you do that?"

She looked at Imhof. He spoke. "It certainly should be done. Obviously. I should have thought of it myself. Will you get the man and woman?"

"If desired, yes. They should also search any other premises with which Miss Wynn has had close association. You have no agent, Miss Wynn?"

"No."

"Have you ever had one?"

"No." Again the little flush. *"Knock at My Door* is my first novel—my first published one. Before that I had only had a few stories in magazines, and no agent would take me—at least no good one. This has been a big shock, Mr. Wolfe—my first book such a big success, and you can imagine I was up riding the clouds, and then all of a sudden this—this awful business."

Wolfe nodded. "No doubt. Do you own a motor car?"

"Yes. I bought one last month."

"It must be searched. What else? Do you have a locker at a tennis court?"

"No. Nothing like that."

"Do you frequently spend the night away from your home? Fairly frequently?"

I expected that to bring a bigger and better flush, but apparently her mind was purer than mine. She shook her head. "Almost never. I'm not a very social creature, Mr. Wolfe. I guess I really have no intimate friends. My only close relatives, my father and mother, live in Montana, and I haven't been there for ten years. You said they should search any premises with which I have had close association, but there aren't any."

Wolfe's head turned. "As I told you on the phone, Mr. Harvey, I know nothing about plagiarism, but I would have supposed that it concerned an infringement of copyright. All five of these claims were based on material that had not been published and so were not protected by copyright. Why were the claims not merely ignored?"

"They couldn't be," Harvey said. "It's not that simple. I'm not a lawyer, and if you want it in legal terms you can get it from the NAAD counsel, but there's a property right, I believe they call it, in these things even if they haven't been copyrighted. It was in a court trial before a judge that a jury awarded Jane Ogilvy a hundred and thirty-five thousand dollars. Do you want me to get our counsel on the phone?"

"That can wait. First I need to know what you want to hire me to do. The first three cases are history, and apparently the fourth, Mr. Oshin's, soon will be. Do you want me to investigate on behalf of Miss Wynn?"

"No. I should say, yes and no. This committee was set up six weeks ago, before the claim on Miss Wynn was made. It had been authorized at a meeting of the NAAD council in March. It seemed fairly obvious to us what had happened. Alice Porter's putting the squeeze on Ellen Sturdevant, and getting away with it, had started a ball rolling. Her method was copied exactly by Simon Jacobs with Richard Echols, except for one detail, the way he established the priority of his manuscript and the assumption of Echols' access to it; and he changed that one detail because he actually had sent a novelette to that literary agency, Norris and Baum, and had it returned. He merely took advantage of something that had happened two years back. Of course the manuscript which was the basis of his claim —the one he allowed Title House and Echols to inspect —was not the one he had sent to Norris and Baum in nineteen fifty-four. He had written it after Echols' novel had been published and gave it the same title as the one he had sent to Norris and Baum—'What's Mine Is Yours.'"

Wolfe grunted. "You may omit the obvious. You are assuming, I take it, that that was the procedure in all five cases: plagiarism upside down. The manuscript supporting the claim was written after the book was published or the play produced and had achieved success."

"Certainly," Harvey agreed. "That was the pattern. The third one, Jane Ogilvy, followed it exactly, the only difference being that she had a stroke of luck. Whatever plan she had for discovery of the manuscript in Marjorie Lippin's home, she didn't have to use it, for Mrs. Lippin conveniently died. Again, with Kenneth Rennert, the only difference was the way the manuscript was found."

He stopped to cover his mouth with his palm, and a noise came, too feeble to be called a belch. "Sausage for breakfast," he said, for the record. "I shouldn't. That's how it stood when this committee had its first meeting. At the NAAD council meeting a prominent novelist had said that he had a new book scheduled for early fall and he hoped to God it would be a flop, and nobody laughed. At the first meeting of this committee Gerald Knapp, president of Knapp and Bowen—How did you put it, Mr. Knapp?"

Knapp passed his tongue over his lips. "I said that it hasn't hit us yet, but we have three novels on the best-seller list, and we hate to open our mail."

"So that's the situation," Harvey told Wolfe. "And now Alice Porter is repeating. Something has to be done. It has to be stopped. About a dozen lawyers have been consulted, authors' and publishers' lawyers, and none of them has an idea that is worth a damn. Except one maybe—the one who suggested that we put it up to you. Can you stop it?"

Wolfe shook his head. "You don't mean that, Mr. Harvey."

"I don't mean what?"

"That question. If you expect me to say no, you wouldn't have come. If you expect me to say yes, you must think me a swaggerer, and again you wouldn't have come. I certainly wouldn't undertake to make it impossible for anyone ever again to extort money from an author by the stratagem you have described."

"We wouldn't expect you to."

"Then what would you expect?"

"We would expect you to do something about this situation that would make us pay your bill not only because we had to but also because we felt that you had earned it and we had got our money's worth."

Wolfe nodded. "That's more like it. That was phrased as might be expected from the author of *Why the Gods Laugh*, which I have just read. I had been thinking that you write better than you talk, but you put that well because you had been challenged. Do you want to hire me on those terms?"

Harvey looked at Gerald Knapp, and then at Dexter. They looked at each other. Reuben Imhof asked Wolfe, "Could you give us some idea of how you would go about it and what your fee would be?"

"No, sir," Wolfe told him.

"What the hell," Mortimer Oshin said, squashing a cigarette, "he couldn't guarantee anything anyway, could he?"

"I would vote for proceeding on those terms," Gerald Knapp said, "providing it is understood that we can terminate the arrangement at any time."

"That sounds like a clause in a book contract," Harvey said. "Will you accept it, Mr. Wolfe?"

"Certainly."

"Then you're in favor, Mr. Knapp?"

"Yes. It was our attorney who suggested coming to Nero Wolfe."

"Miss Wynn?"

"Yes, if the others are. That was a good idea, having my apartment searched, and the one on Perry Street."

"Mr. Oshin?"

"Sure."

"Mr. Dexter?"

"With the understanding that we can terminate at will, yes."

"Mr. Imhof?"

Imhof had his head cocked. "I'm willing to go along, but I'd like to mention a couple of points. Mr. Wolfe says he can't give us any idea of how he'll go about it, and naturally we can't expect him to pull a rabbit out of a hat here and now, but, as he said himself, the first three cases are history and the fourth one soon will be. But Miss Wynn's isn't. It's hot. The claim has just been made, and it was made by Alice Porter, the woman who started it. So I think he should concentrate on that. My second point is this, if he does concentrate on Alice Porter, and if he gets her, if he makes her withdraw the claim, I think Miss Wynn might feel that it would be fair and proper for her to pay part of Mr. Wolfe's fee. Don't you think so, Amy?"

"Why—yes." Her nose twitched. "Of course."

"It might also," Harvey put in, "be fair and proper for the Victory Press to pay part. Don't you think so?"

"We will." Imhof grinned at him. "We'll contribute to the BPA's share. We might even kick in a little extra." He went to Wolfe. "How about concentrating on Alice Porter?"

"I may do that, sir. Upon consideration." Wolfe focused on the chairman. "Who is my client? Not this committee."

"Well . . ." Harvey looked at Gerald Knapp. Knapp smiled and spoke. "The arrangement, Mr. Wolfe, is that the Book Publishers of America and the National Association of Authors and Dramatists will each pay half of any expenses incurred by this committee. They are your clients. You will report to Mr. Harvey, the committee chairman, as their agent. I trust that is satisfactory?"

"Yes. This may be a laborious and costly operation, and I must ask for an advance against expenses. Say five thousand dollars?"

Knapp looked at Harvey. Harvey said, "All right. You'll get it."

"Very well." Wolfe straightened up, took a deep breath, and let it out. It looked as if he were going to have to dig in and do a little work, and it takes a lot of oxygen to face a prospect as dismal as that. "Naturally," he said, "I must have all records and documents pertaining to all of the cases, or copies of them. Everything. Including, for instance, the reports from the detective agency hired by Mr. Oshin. I can form no plan until I am fully informed, but it may help to get answers to a few questions now. Mr. Harvey. Has any effort been made to discover a connection among Alice Porter, Simon Jacobs, Jane Ogilvy, and Kenneth Rennert, or between any two of them?"

Harvey nodded. "Sure, that's been tried. By the lawyer representing Marjorie Lippin's heirs, her son and daughter, and by the detective agency Oshin hired. They didn't find any."

"Where are the four manuscripts on which the claims were based? Not copies, the manuscripts themselves. Are they available?"

"We have two of them, Alice Porter's 'There Is Only Love' and Simon Jacobs' 'What's Mine Is Yours.' Jane Ogilvy's 'On Earth but Not in Heaven' was an exhibit in evidence at the trial, and after she won the case it was returned to her. We have a copy of it—a copy, not a facsimile. Kenneth Rennert's play outline, 'A Bushel of Love,' is in the possession of Oshin's attorney, and he won't give us a copy of it. Of course we—"

Mortimer Oshin postponed striking a match to mutter, "He won't even let me have a copy."

Harvey finished, "Of course we know nothing about Alice Porter's 'Opportunity Knocks,' the basis of her claim against Amy Wynn. I have a suspicion that you'll find it when you search the apartment Miss Wynn lived in on Perry Street. If you do, then what?"

"I have no idea." Wolfe made a face. "Confound it, you have merely shown me the skeleton, and I am not a wizard. I must know what has been done and what has been overlooked, in each case. What of the paper and typing of the manuscripts? Did they offer no grounds for a challenge? What of the records and backgrounds of the claimants? Did Jane Ogilvy testify at the trial, and was she cross-examined competently? How did Alice Porter's manuscript get into Ellen Sturdevant's bureau drawer? How did Jane Ogilvy's manuscript get into the trunk in Marjorie Lippin's attic? How did Kenneth Rennert's play outline get into the file of Mr. Oshin's former agent? Was any sort of answer found, even a conjectural one, to any of those questions?"

He spread his hands. "And there is the question, what about your assumption that all of the claims were fraudulent? I can't swallow it with my eyes shut. I can accept it as a working hypothesis, but I can't dismiss the possibility that one or more of the supposed victims is a thief and a liar. 'Most writers steal a good thing when they can' is doubtless an—"

"Blah!" Mortimer Oshin exploded.

Wolfe's brows went up. "That was in quotation marks, Mr. Oshin. It was said, or written, more than a century ago by Barry Cornwall, the English poet and dramatist. He wrote *Mirandola*, a tragedy performed at Covent Garden with Macready and Kemble. It is doubtless an exaggeration, but it is not blah. If there had been then in England a National Association of Authors and Dramatists, Barry Cornwall would have been a member. So that question must remain open along with the others."

His eyes moved. "Miss Wynn. The search of the apartments should not be delayed. Will you arrange it, or shall I?"

Amy Wynn looked at Imhof. He told her, "Let him do it." She told Wolfe, "You do it."

"Very well. You will get permission from your former fellow tenants at Perry Street, and you will admit the searchers to your present apartment and then absent yourself. Archie, get Saul Panzer and Miss Bonner."

I turned to the phone and dialed.

Chapter 3

Thirty-four hours later, at eleven o'clock Wednesday evening, Wolfe straightened up in his chair and spoke. "Archie."

My fingers, on the typewriter keys, stopped. "Yes, sir?"

"Another question has been answered."

"Good. Which one?"

"About the candor of the victims. Their bona fides is established. They were swindled. Look here."

I got up and crossed to his desk. To get there I had to detour around a table that had been brought from the front room to hold about half a ton of paper. There were correspondence folders, newspaper clippings, photographs, mimeographed reports, transcripts of telephone conversations, photostats, books, tear sheets, lists of names and addresses, affidavits, and miscellaneous items. With time out only for meals and sleep and his two daily sessions in the plant rooms on the roof, Wolfe had spent the thirty-four hours working through it, and so had I. We had both read all of it except the four books—*The Color of Passion*, by Ellen Sturdevant, *Hold Fast to All I Give You*, by Richard Echols, *Sacred or Profane*, by Marjorie Lippin, and

Knock at My Door, by Amy Wynn. There was no point in wading through them, since it was acknowledged that their plots and characters and action were the same as those in the stories on which the claims had been based.

What I was typing, when he interrupted me, was a statement to be signed by Saul Panzer and Dol Bonner, who had come late that afternoon to report. Tuesday afternoon and evening they had spent seven hours at the apartment on Perry Street, and six hours Wednesday at Amy Wynn's current apartment on Arbor Street. They were prepared to swear on a stack of best-sellers that in neither place was there a manuscript of a story by Alice Porter entitled "Opportunity Knocks." At Perry Street there had been no manuscript at all, by anybody. At Arbor Street there had been a drawerful of them—two novels, twenty-eight stories, and nine articles—all by Amy Wynn and all showing signs of the wear and tear that comes from a series of trips through the mails. Saul had made a list of the titles and number of pages, but I had decided it wasn't necessary to include it in the statement. I had dialed Philip Harvey's number to report to the chairman, but there was no answer, so I had called Reuben Imhof at Victory Press. He was glad to get the good news and said he would tell Amy Wynn.

Having detoured around the table with its load of paper, I stood at the end of Wolfe's desk. Ranged before him were three of the items of the collection: the manuscripts of Alice Porter's "There Is Only Love," and Simon Jacobs' "What's Mine Is Yours," and the copy of Jane Ogilvy's "On Earth but Not in Heaven." In his hand were some sheets from his scratch pad. His elbow was on the chair arm with his forearm perpendicular. It takes energy to hold a forearm straight up, and he only does it when he is especially pleased with himself.

"I'm looking," I said. "What is it? Fingerprints?"

"Better than fingerprints. These three stories were all written by the same person."

"Yeah? Not on the same typewriter. I compared them with a glass."

"So did I." He rattled the sheets. "Better than a typewriter. A typewriter can change hands." He glanced at the top sheet. "In Alice Porter's story a character avers something six times. In Simon Jacobs' story, eight times. In Jane Ogilvy's story, seven times. You know, of course, that nearly every writer of dialogue has his pet substitute, or substitutes, for 'say.' Wanting a variation for 'he said' or 'she said,' they have him declare, state, blurt, spout, cry, pronounce, avow, murmur, mutter, snap—there are dozens of them; and they tend to repeat the same one. Would you accept it as coincidence that this man and those two women have the same favorite, 'aver'?"

"Maybe with salt. I heard you say once that it is not inconceivable that the fall in temperature when the sun moves south is merely a coincidence."

"Pfui. That was conversation. This is work. There are other similarities, equally remarkable, in these stories. Two of them are verbal." He looked at the second sheet. "Alice Porter has this: 'Not for nothing would he abandon the only person he had ever loved.' And this: 'She might lose her self-respect, but not for nothing.' Simon Jacobs has this: 'And must he forfeit his honor too? Not for nothing:' And this: 'Not for nothing had she suffered tortures that no woman could be expected to survive.' Jane Ogilvy has a man say in reply to a question, 'Not for nothing, my dear, not for nothing.'"

I scratched my cheek. "Well. Not for nothing did you read the stories."

He went to the third sheet. "Another verbal one. Alice Porter has this: 'Barely had she touched him when he felt his heart pounding.' And this: 'Night had barely fallen by the time she reached the door and got out her key.' And this: 'Was there still a chance? Barely a chance?' Simon Jacobs used 'barely' four times, in similar constructions, and Jane Ogilvy three times."

"I'm sold," I averred. "Coincidence is out."

"But there are two others. One is punctuation. They are all fond of semicolons and use them where most people would prefer a comma or a dash. The other is more subtle but to me the most conclusive. A clever man might successfully disguise every element of his style but one—the paragraphing. Diction and syntax may be determined and controlled by rational processes in full consciousness, but paragraphing—the decision whether to take short hops or long ones, whether to hop in the middle of a thought or action or finish it first—that comes from instinct, from the depths of personality. I will concede the possibility that the verbal similarities, and even the punctuation, could be coincidence, though it is highly improbable; but not the paragraphing. These three stories were paragraphed by the same person."

"Plot it yourself," I said.

"What?"

"Nothing. The title of a piece I happened to read in the *Times Book Review* just popped up. It was about the idea that a novelist should just create his characters and let them go ahead and develop the action and the plot. This guy was dead against it. He claimed you should plot it yourself. I was thinking that a detective working on a case can't plot it himself. It has already been plotted. Look at this. This is now a totally different animal. One thing: with all those similarities, why hasn't anyone noticed it?"

"Probably because no one has ever had the three manuscripts together and compared them. Until that committee was formed they were in different hands."

I returned to my desk and sat. "Okay. Congratulations. So I'll have to rearrange my mind. I suppose you already have."

"No. I hadn't even arranged it."

I glanced up at the clock. "Quarter past eleven. Harvey might be home. Do you want to swagger?"

"No. I'm tired. I want to sleep. There's no hurry." He pushed his chair back and got to his feet.

Sometimes he self-propels his seventh of a ton up one flight of stairs to his room, but that night he used the elevator. When he had gone I took the three stories to my desk and spent half an hour studying paragraphing, and though Lily Rowan told me once that I am about as subtle as a sledge hammer—at a moment when her diction was not determined and controlled by rational processes in full consciousness—I saw what Wolfe meant. I put the stories in the safe and then considered the problem of the table-load of paper. The statuses and functions of the inhabitants of that old brownstone on West 35th Street are clearly understood. Wolfe is the owner and the commandant. Fritz Brenner is the chef and housekeeper and is responsible for the condition of the castle with the exception of the plant rooms, the office, and my bedroom. Theodore Horstmann is the orchid-tender, with no responsibilities or business on the lower floors. He eats in the kitchen with Fritz. I eat in the dining room with Wolfe, except when we are not speaking; then I join

Fritz and Theodore in the kitchen, or get invited somewhere, or take a friend to a restaurant, or go to Bert's
diner around the corner on Tenth Avenue and eat
beans. My status and function are whatever a given
situation calls for, and the question who decides what
it calls for is what occasionally creates an atmosphere
in which Wolfe and I are not speaking. The next sentence is to be, "But the table-load of paper, being in
the office, was clearly up to me," and I have to decide
whether to put it here or start a new paragraph with
it. You see how subtle it is. Paragraph it yourself.

I stood surveying the stacks of paper. Scattered
through them were assorted items of information
about the four claimants. Assuming that one of them
had written the stories, which was the most likely can-
didate? I ran over them in my mind.

Alice Porter. In her middle thirties, unmarried. No
physical description, but a photograph. Fleshy, say 150
pounds. Round face, small nose, eyes too close together. In 1955 had lived at Collander House on West
82nd Street, a hive-home for girls and women who
couldn't afford anything fancy. Was now living near
Carmel, sixty miles north of New York, in a cottage
which she had presumably bought with some of the
loot she had pried out of Ellen Sturdevant. Between
1949 and 1955 had had fourteen stories for children
published in magazines, and one children's book, *The
Moth That Ate Peanuts*, published by Best and Green
in 1954, not a success. Joined the National Association
of Authors and Dramatists in 1951, was dropped for
nonpayment of dues in 1954, rejoined in 1956.

Simon Jacobs. Description and photograph. Sixty-
two years old, thin and scrawny, hair like Mark
Twain's (that item from Title House's lawyer), stut-
tered. Married in 1948, therefore at the age of fifty-

one. In 1956 was living with his wife and three children in a tenement on West 21st Street, and was still there. Overseas with AEF in First World War, wounded twice: Wrote hundreds of stories for the pulps between 1922 and 1940, using four pen names. Was with the OWI in the Second World War, writing radio scripts in German and Polish. After the war wrote stories again, but didn't sell so many, eight or ten a year at three cents a word. In 1947 had a book published by the Owl Press, *Barrage at Dawn*, of which 35,000 copies were sold, and got married in 1948 and took an apartment in Brooklyn Heights. No more books published. Fewer stories sold. In 1954 moved to the tenement on West 21st Street. Member of the NAAD since 1931, dues always paid promptly, even during the war when he didn't have to.

Jane Ogilvy. Descriptions from three sources and several photographs. Late twenties or early thirties, depending on the source. Nice little figure, pretty little face, dreamy-eyed. In 1957 was living with her parents in their house in Riverdale, and still was. Went to Europe alone immediately after she collected from Marjorie Lippin's estate, but only stayed a month. Her father was in wholesale hardware, high financial rating. She had testified in court that she had had seventeen poems published in magazines, and had read three of them on the witness stand at the request of her attorney. No stories or books published. Member of the NAAD since 1955; was behind a year on her dues.

Kenneth Rennert. I could supply several pages on him, from the reports of the detective agency hired by Mortimer Oshin. Thirty-four years old, single. Looked younger. Virile (not my word, the detective's), muscular, handsome. Piercing brown eyes and so on. Living in a nice big room with bath and kitchenette on East 37th Street; the detective had combed it twice. Had mother and sisters in Ottumwa, Iowa; father dead. Graduated from Princeton in 1950. Got a job with a brokerage house, Orcutt and Company, was discharged in 1954 for cause, exact cause not ascertained, but it was something about diddling customers. No public charges. Began writing for television. So far as could be learned had sold only nine scripts in four years, but no other known source of income. Has borrowed money right and left; probably owes thirty or forty grand. Never a member of the NAAD; not eligible. Has never submitted a play to an agent or producer.

There they were. My guess, just to sleep on, was Alice Porter. She had worked it first, back in 1955, and was now repeating. She had written a book entitled *The Moth That Ate Peanuts*, which showed that she would stop at nothing. Her eyes were too close together. My suggestion in the morning, if Wolfe asked for one, as he usually did just to be polite, would be to connect her up with Simon Jacobs in 1956, Jane Ogilvy in 1957, and possibly Kenneth Rennert in 1958. If she had written the stories and they had used them, there had certainly been contacts. Oshin's detective agency and the lawyer for Marjorie Lippin's estate hadn't found any, but whether something is found or not depends on who is looking for it.

Making room on the shelves of one of the cabinets, I lugged the stuff from the table to it, seven trips, locked the cabinet, returned the table to the front room, and went up to bed.

Chapter 4

I never made that suggestion because I slept it off.
I had a better one. At 8:15 Thursday morning I
descended two flights, entered the kitchen, exchanged good mornings with Fritz, picked up my ten-
ounce glass of orange juice, took that first sour-sweet
sip, which is always the first hint that the fog is going
to lift, and inquired, "No omelet?"

Fritz shut the refrigerator door. "You well know,
Archie, what it means when the eggs are not broken."

"Sure, but I'm hungry."

It meant that when Fritz had taken Wolfe's breakfast tray up to his room he had been told that I was
wanted, and he would not break eggs until he heard
me coming down again. I will not gulp orange juice, so
after a second sip I took it along—up a flight, left to
the door standing open at the end of the hall, and in.
Wolfe, barefooted, a yellow mountain in his pajamas,
was in his next-to-favorite chair at the table by a window, spooning raspberry jam onto a griddle cake. I
returned his greeting and went on, "Copies of *The
Moth That Ate Peanuts* and *Barrage at Dawn* are
probably available at the publishers', but it might take
days to dig up the magazines with Jane Ogilvy's po-

ems. Also will the books be enough for Alice Porter and Simon Jacobs, or will you want some stories too?"

He grunted. "No special sagacity was required."

"No, sir. I'm not swaggering. It's just that I'm hungry and wanted to save time."

"You have. First the books. No stories may be needed. Jane Ogilvy's poems would almost certainly be worthless; I have read three of them. A writer of gimcrack verse chooses words only to scan and rhyme, and there is no paragraphing."

I sipped orange juice. "If they want to know why we want the books, do I explain?"

"No. Evade." He forked a bite of cake and jam.

"What if Harvey calls?"

"We have nothing to report. Possibly later. I want those books."

"Anything else?"

"No." He lifted the fork and opened his mouth.

When I got back to the kitchen Fritz had broken the eggs and was stirring. I sat at the table by the wall, propped the morning *Times* on the rack, and sipped orange juice. Fritz asked, "A good case?"

For him a good case is one which will not interfere with meals, will not last long enough to make Wolfe cranky, and will probably produce a nice fat fee. "So-so," I told him. "All we have to do is read a couple of books. Maybe."

He put the skillet on. "That Miss Bonner is helping?"

I grinned at him. He regards every woman who enters the house as a potential threat to his kitchen, not to mention the rest of his precinct, and he was particularly suspicious of Dol Bonner, Dol being short for Theodolinda, the only female owner and operator of a detective agency in New York. "No," I said, "she came yesterday on a personal matter. Mr. Wolfe keeps phoning her to ask her to dinner, and she wants me to get him to stop annoying her."

He pointed the spoon at me. "Archie, if I could lie with your aplomb I would be an ambassador. You know women. You know quite well that one with eyes the color of that Miss Bonner and eyelashes of that length, her own, is a dangerous animal."

By nine o'clock the morning fog had gone entirely, thanks to the apricot omelet, griddle cakes with bacon and honey, and two cups of coffee, and I went to the office and dialed Philip Harvey's number. From his reaction you might have thought it was not yet dawn. After smoothing him down and promising never to call him again earlier than noon, short of a real emergency, I told him what I wanted—the names of people at Best and Green and the Owl Press who could be expected to cooperate. He said he knew no one at either place, told me to call the executive secretary of NAAD, and hung up. A hell of a chairman. When I got the executive secretary she wanted to know what kind of cooperation I was going to ask for. I told her, and she wanted to know why Nero Wolfe wanted the books. I said that no good detective ever tells anybody why he wants something, and if I gave her a reason it would be a phony, and I finally wore her down and got a couple of names.

Mr. Arnold Green of Best and Green was extremely suspicious. He didn't come right out with it, but I gathered that he suspected that the Joint Committee on Plagiarism was a conspiracy, abetted by some of his competitors, to twist the nose of Best and Green by getting something on an author whose book they had published five years ago; and anyway, *The Moth That Ate Peanuts* was a flop and had been remaindered, and the only copies they had left, maybe four or five, were in the morgue. And more anyway, what did that book have to do with the investigation Nero Wolfe was making? When he had simmered down a little I said I fully appreciated his point of view, and I would tell Mr. Knapp and Mr. Dexter and Mr. Imhof that for some reason, probably a good one, he refused to send Mr. Wolf a copy of the book, and he said I misunderstood, that he wasn't refusing, that there might possibly be a copy somewhere around the office. If so he would send it down by messenger, and if not he would send someone to the morgue for one.

Mr. W. R. Pratt of the Owl Press was strictly business. When I said that Nero Wolfe had been hired to make an investigation by the Joint Committee on Plag—he cut in to say he knew that and what did I want; and when I said that Mr. Wolfe wanted a copy of *Barrage at Dawn* as soon as possible and would be obliged if he would kindly—he cut in again to say that if I would give the address to his secretary she would send it at once by messenger. He asked no questions, but his secretary did. Her first words were, "Whom do we bill?" That outfit was right on its toes.

Barrage at Dawn arrived first, which didn't surprise me, with an invoice enclosed which included an item of $1.50 for messenger service. Wolfe had come down from the plant rooms and was looking through the morning's mail. When I handed him the book he made a face at it and dropped it on his desk, but in a couple of minutes he picked it up, frowned at the cover, and opened it. He was well into it when *The Moth That Ate Peanuts* arrived, and since, as I said, my function is whatever an occasion calls for, I tackled that one, looking for "aver" or "not for nothing" or something like "Barely had the moth swallowed the

ten-thousandth peanut when it got a stomach-ache."
Also, of course, semicolons and paragraphing. I was
more than halfway through when Wolfe asked for it,
and I got up and handed it to him and took *Barrage at
Dawn.*

A little after one, with lunchtime approaching,
Wolfe shut *The Moth That Ate Peanuts*, tossed it onto
his desk, and growled, "Pfui. Neither one. Confound
it."

I closed *Barrage at Dawn* and put it down. "I can
see," I said, "that you might cross Simon Jacobs off,
but Alice Porter's is a children's book. You wouldn't
expect a moth to aver, even if it was a peanut addict. I
would hate to give up Alice Porter. She started it and
she's repeating."

He glared at me. "No. She didn't write those stories."

"If you say so. Why glare at me? I didn't write
them. Is this final or are you just sore because he or
she was smart enough to wear gloves?"

"It's final. No one is that smart. Those two are
eliminated."

"Then that leaves Jane Ogilvy and Kenneth Rennert."

"Jane Ogilvy is highly unlikely. The woman who
wrote those three pseudo-poems and used the terms
and locutions that appear in her testimony at the trial
is almost certainly incapable of writing those three
stories, including the one that she claimed she had
written. Kenneth Rennert is of course a possibility,
the only one left of the quartet. But his claim is based
on a play outline, not a story, and we don't have it. It
might even be that his was an independent operation.
Could we get copies of the television scripts he has
written?"

"I don't know. Shall I find out?"

"Yes, but there is no urgency. According to that report, they were dramatic in form and so contained nothing but dialogue, and would tell us next to nothing. I would like your opinion. Our job now is to find a person, man or woman: the person who in nineteen fifty-five read *The Color of Passion*, by Ellen Sturdevant, wrote a story with the title 'There Is Only Love,' incorporating its characters and plot and action, persuaded Alice Porter to use it as the basis for a claim of plagiarism, putting her name on it, the bait being presumably a share of the proceeds, and at an opportune moment somehow entered the summer home of Ellen Sturdevant and concealed the manuscript in a bureau drawer; who repeated the performance a year later with *Hold Fast to All I Give You*, by Richard Echols, using another accomplice, Simon Jacobs, changing only the method of establishing the existence and priority of the manuscript, suggested by the convenient circumstance that Jacobs had once sent a story to Echols' agent and had it returned; who in nineteen fifty-seven again repeated the performance with *Sacred or Profane*, by Marjorie Lippin, using still another accomplice, Jane Ogilvy, following the same pattern, with the advantage of another convenient circumstance, the death of Marjorie Lippin. I would like your opinion. Is Kenneth Rennert that person?"

I shook my head. "I don't know him well enough."

"You have read that report."

"Yeah." I considered. "Offhand I would vote no. One will get you ten that he isn't. From the general impression I got of him. Especially I doubt if he would monkey around with accomplices. A specific point: There is no evidence that he had any connection with writing or writers until he took a shot at television in nineteen fifty-five, so how did he get on to Alice Porter and Jacobs and Jane Ogilvy? Another one: If he used them on the first three, splitting the take with them, because he didn't want to do it himself, why did he do it himself for the fourth and then go back to Alice Porter for the fifth?"

Wolfe nodded. "I agree. We are caught in our own noose. By discovering that those three stories were written by the same person we thought we had simplified the problem. It now appears that we have complicated it. If those four were merely cat's-paws, where is the monkey? He is presumably a United States citizen. There are a hundred and seventy million of them."

"It's not that bad," I averred. "He's probably in the metropolitan area. Fifteen million. Not counting children, illiterates, millionaires, people in jail—"

Fritz had appeared at the door. "Lunch is ready, sir."

"I have no appetite," Wolfe growled.

It was off a little. He only ate four Creole fritters with cheese sauce instead of the usual five.

Chapter 5

So he pulled a mutiny, the first one in three years. His mutinies are like other people's. Other people mutiny against the Army or Navy or some other authority, but he mutinies against himself. It was his house and his office, and he had taken the job, but now he turned his back on it. His discovery that the three stories had all been written by one person, which I admit was fairly neat, had backfired on him, and he quit. Of course business is never mentioned at the table, but from his mood I knew he was smoldering, so when we returned to the office after lunch I asked politely whether there would be instructions then or later.

"Now," he said. "You will see, at your convenience and theirs, Miss Porter, Miss Ogilvy, Mr. Jacobs, and Mr. Rennert. In whatever order you prefer. Make their acquaintance."

I stayed polite. "It will be a pleasure to meet them. What are we to talk about?"

"Whatever occurs to you. I have never known you to be short of words."

"How about bringing them, one at a time, to make *your* acquaintance?"

"No."

"I see." I stood and looked down at him. That annoys him because he has to tilt his head to look up. "It must be wonderful to be a genius. Like that singer, Doria Ricco, whenever anything goes wrong she just walks out. Then she has a press conference. Shall I set one up for six o'clock? You could tell them that a great artist like you can't be expected to take a setback which any ordinary detective would only—"

"You will please keep your remarks to yourself."

So it was a mutiny, not just a passing peeve. If he had merely barked at me "Shut up!" as he does two or three times a week, I would have known he would snap out of it in an hour or so and go to work, but that was bad. It would take time, no telling how much. And he left his chair, crossed to the bookshelves, took a volume of Shakespeare from the set, returned to his seat, leaned back, and opened the book. Bowing out not only from the case, but from the country and the century. I went. Leaving the room and the house, I walked to Ninth Avenue and flagged a taxi and told the driver 632 West 21st Street.

That building was a tenement not only as defined in the New York Tenement House Act, but also as what people usually mean when they say "tenement." It was a dump. Having decided in the taxi how to start a conversation with Simon Jacobs, I found his name in the row, next to the top, and pressed the button. When the click sounded I pushed the door open, entered, and went to the stairs and started up, smelling garlic. The smell of garlic in Spanish sauce as Fritz makes it is a come-on, but in a tenement hall where it has been seeping into the plaster for fifty years it's a pinch-nose. The best way is to pull in a long deep breath of it immediately and then your insides know it's hopeless.

Three flights up a woman was standing at an open door near the front of the hall, with a boy, nine or ten, at her elbow. As I approached, the boy said, "Oh, it's not Tommy," and disappeared. I asked the woman, "Mrs. Jacobs?"

She nodded. She was a surprise. Simon Jacobs, now sixty-two, had been fifty-one when he had married in 1948, but she was no crone. There wasn't a wrinkle showing, and there was no sign of gray in her soft brown hair. When I told her my name and I would like to speak with her husband, and she said he didn't like to be disturbed when he was working and would I please tell her what I wanted, and I said I wasn't selling anything, it was a business matter and might be to his advantage, she turned and went, leaving the door open. After a long moment he appeared, a good likeness to the photograph—thin and scrawny, with enough wrinkles for two, and, as Title House's lawyer had said, hair like Mark Twain's.

"Well, sir?" A thin high voice would have fitted him, but his was deep and full.

"My name's Goodwin, Mr. Jacobs."

"So my wife said."

"I'm on the staff of a magazine with national circulation. I won't name it until I find out if you're interested in an idea we are considering. May I come in?"

"That depends. I'm right in the middle of a story. I don't want to be rude, but what's the idea?"

"Well—we thought we might ask you to do an article for us. About how it feels to have a story you have written stolen by another author and turned into a best-seller. We thought 'Plot It Yourself' might be a good title for it. I'd like to tell you how we think it might be handled, and we can discuss—"

He shut the door in my face. You may think I'm not

much of a detective, that an experienced snoop should have had sense enough to have it blocked with his foot, but in the first place it was totally unexpected, and in the second place you don't block a door unless you're on the offensive. So I merely put my thumb to my nose and wiggled my fingers, turned, and made for the stairs. When I got to the sidewalk I took a long, deep breath to let my insides know they could relax. Then I walked to Tenth Avenue, stopped a taxi, and told the driver 37th and Lexington.

That building, between Lexington and Third, was a house of a different color. It may have been nearly as old as the 21st Street tenement, but it had used make-up. Its brick front was painted silver-gray with bright blue trim, the doorframe was aluminum, and there were evergreens in boxes. There were eight names on the panel in the vestibule, two tenants to a floor, with a grill to talk through and a receiver on a hook. I pushed the button opposite Rennert and put the receiver to my ear, and in a moment had a crackle and then a voice.

"Who is it?"

"You don't know me. My name's Goodwin. Nothing to sell. I may want to buy something."

"Bill Goodwin?"

"No. Archie Goodwin."

"Archie? Not by any chance Nero Wolfe's Archie Goodwin?"

"In person."

"Well, well! I often wonder what detectives buy one-half so precious as the goods they sell. Come on up and tell me! Top floor."

I hung up and turned, and when the buzz sounded opened the door and entered. More aluminum, framing the self-service elevator. I stepped in and pushed the

"4" button and was lifted. When it stopped and the door opened he was there in the little hall, shirt sleeves rolled up and no tie, virile, muscular, handsome, looking younger than thirty-four. I took his offered hand and returned his manly grip and was ushered through a door and was in the nice big room. It was even nicer and bigger than the report had led me to expect. He had me take a nice big chair and asked, "Scotch, rye, bourbon, gin?"

I declined with thanks, and he sat on a nice big couch which probably doubled as a bed. "This is a pleasure," he said, "unless you want my fingerprints to compare them with the ones you found on the dagger that was sticking in the back of the corpse. I swear I didn't do it. I always stab people in front. I like that suit. Matthew Jonas?"

I told him no, Peter Darrell. "Fingerprints wouldn't help," I said. "There were none on the dagger. It was one of those old Arabian antiques with a fancy handle. What I told you was straight. I may want to buy something—or rather, a client of Nero Wolfe's may. He's a guy with money who wants more. He gets ideas. He has the idea that he might like to buy your claim against Mortimer Oshin and Al Friend for stealing your play outline, 'A Bushel of Love,' and turning it into *A Barrel of Love*. He might pay ten thousand cash for an assignment of the claim and your affidavit supporting it, and another ten thousand if and when Oshin and Friend pay up. Of course he would expect you to testify without a subpoena if it goes to trial."

"Well, well." He stretched a leg on the couch. "Who is this fairy godfather?"

"A client of Mr. Wolfe's. We handled a problem for

him once, not this kind. If we agree on a deal you'll meet him. The ten thousand is ready in bills."

"What if they never pay up?"

"That's his risk. He would be out ten grand."

"Nuts. They'll pay. They'll pay ten times ten. At least."

"Possibly," I conceded. "Some day. If it goes to trial, there'll be lawyers' fees and other expenses."

"Well." He put his other leg up. "Tell him I might be interested. I'm willing to meet him and discuss it with him."

I shook my head. "I'm here to discuss it. The reason he got Mr. Wolfe to handle it, there are a couple of little details to arrange. For one, he would like to have some evidence in his possession that that's not the only dramatic plot you ever hatched. That should be easy. I suppose you have copies of some of your television scripts."

"Sure. All of them."

"Fine. That would settle that. The other one, if it gets to court, it would help a lot to have some backing for your testimony that you wrote the outline with your name on it that was found in Jack Sandler's office files, and the best backing would be to produce the typewriter that you wrote it on. Our client would want it. Of course he would pay you for it."

"That would be sweet of him."

"He's not sweet. Between you and me, I don't like him."

"Neither do I. He stole my play." His legs swung around and he was on his feet. "All right, Hawkshaw. Beat it."

I stayed put. "Now listen, Mr. Rennert. I can understand how you—"

"I said beat it." He took a step. "Do you want help?"

I arose and took two steps, and was facing him at arm's length. "Would you like to try?"

I was hoping he would. Wolfe's mutiny had put me in a humor that would have made it a pleasure to take a swing at somebody, and this character was the right size and build to make it not only a pleasure but good exercise. He didn't oblige me. His eyes stayed with mine, but he backed up a foot.

"I don't want to get blood on the rug," he said.

I turned and went. As I was opening the door he called to my back, "Tell Mortimer Oshin this is like one of his lousy plots!" The elevator was still there, and I stepped in and pushed the button.

On the sidewalk I looked at my wrist: 4:05. Carmel was only a ninety-minute drive, and it would be good for my nerves, but I would phone first. What was Alice Porter's number? I stood at the curb and closed my eyes and concentrated, and dug it out of the cell that had filed it. Around the corner on Lexington Avenue I found a booth, dialed, counted fourteen rings, and hung up. No answer. I settled for a shorter drive. I hoofed it crosstown to Tenth Avenue and a block south to the garage, got the Heron sedan, which was Wolfe's by purchase but mine by mandate, and headed for the West Side Highway.

It was now twenty to one in my book, or maybe thirty to one, that Kenneth Rennert was not it. Whoever had planned and handled the campaign, writing the stories and picking the accomplices and taking advantage of the different circumstances for planting the manuscripts, was no fumbler, but Rennert was. Having suspected, or decided, that Mortimer Oshin was Wolfe's client and I was trying to slip one over, which had not required any strain on the brain, if he had been half smart he would have played me along instead of bouncing me. He was just one of the chorus, not the star. I had filed him away by the time I left the Henry Hudson Parkway at Exit Eleven.

Riverdale, whose streets were planned by someone who couldn't stand the idea of a straight line, is a jungle for a stranger, but I had a good map and only had to turn around twice on my way to 78 Haddon Place. Rolling to the curb in front, I gave it a look. There was too much bigger stuff, everything from tulip beds up to full-grown trees, to leave much room for lawns, but what grass there was would have been fine for putting practice. The house was stone up to your chin and then dark brown wood with the boards running up and down instead of horizontal. Very classy. I got out and started up the walk.

Hearing music as I neared the entrance, I stopped and cocked an ear. Not from inside; from the left. I took to the grass, rounded a corner of the house, passed a row of windows, turned another corner, and stepped onto a flagged terrace. The music, coming from a portable radio on a chair, had an audience of one: Jane Ogilvy. She was stretched out on a mat, on her back, with none of her skin covered except minimum areas at the two vital spots. Her eyes were closed. The deduction I had made from the photographs, in which she had been dressed, that she had a nice little figure, was confirmed. She even had good knees.

I was deciding whether to retreat around the corner and make another approach with sound effects, or stay put and cough, when her eyes suddenly opened and her head turned. She squinted at me five seconds and spoke. "I knew someone had come. The felt presence though not perceived. You're real, I suppose?"

It was strange. It wasn't like a hunch; it was more as if I had asked a question and she had answered it. When Wolfe had eliminated her because of her testimony at the trial and the three poems she had read, I had had my doubts, but those few words from her settled it. If Rennert was now thirty to one, she was a thousand to one.

"Don't speak," she said, "even if you're real. There's nothing you could say that would be worthy of the moment when I felt you here. You may think I heard you, but I didn't. My ears were filled with the music, all of me was, when I felt you. If it were the Eve of Saint Agnes—but it isn't, and I am not supperless, and I'm not in bed. . . . But what if your name were Porphyro? Is it—no, don't speak! Are you going to come closer?"

I agreed with her absolutely. There was nothing I could say that would be worthy of the occasion. Besides, my name wasn't Porphyro. But I didn't want to turn and go with no response at all, so I reached to the trellis beside me and picked a red rose, pressed it to my lips, and tossed it to her. Then I went.

At a phone booth in a drugstore a few blocks away I dialed Alice Porter's number in Carmel, and again there was no answer. That left me with nowhere to go and nothing to do. Of course Wolfe's idea in telling me to go and make the acquaintance of the quartet had been simply to get rid of me, since he knew that if I stuck around I would ride him; and even if I didn't ride him I would look at him. So I dialed another number, got an answer, made a suggestion about ways of passing the time for the next eight or nine hours, and had it accepted. Then I dialed the number I knew best and told Fritz I wouldn't be home for dinner. It was well after midnight when I mounted the stoop of the old brownstone on West 35th Street and used my key. There was no note for me on my desk. I left one in the kitchen for Fritz, telling him not to expect me for breakfast until ten o'clock. I can always use eight hours' sleep, and if Wolfe snapped out of it during the night he knew where to find me.

When I went down to breakfast Friday morning I had a packed bag with me, and at a quarter to eleven I took my second cup of coffee to the office, to my desk, and buzzed the plant rooms on the house phone. Wolfe's voice came. "Yes?"

"Good morning." I was cheerful. "You may remember that I have accepted an invitation for the weekend."

"Yes."

"Should I call it off?"

"No."

"Then I have a suggestion. I saw three of them yesterday, Jacobs and Rennert and Miss Ogilvy, but not Alice Porter. She didn't answer her phone. As you know, Miss Rowan's place, where I'm going, is near Katonah, and it's less than half an hour from there to Carmel. Miss Rowan expects me at six o'clock. If I leave now I can go to Carmel first and have the afternoon for making the acquaintance of Miss Porter."

"Is there anything in the mail that requires attention?"

"No. Nothing that can't wait."

"Then go."

"Right. I'll be back late Sunday evening. Do you want a report on the three I saw before I go?"

"No. If you had anything exigent to report you would have said so."

"Sure. Miss Rowan's phone number is on your desk. I'll give her your regards. Don't overdo."

He hung up. The big fat bum. I wrote the phone number on his memo pad, went to the kitchen to tell Fritz good-by, got my bag, and was gone.

There is always traffic on the West Side Highway, twenty-four hours a day, but it thinned out beyond the city limits, and north of Hawthorne Circle I had long stretches to myself. After leaving Route 22 at Croton Falls and meandering through patches of woods and along shores of reservoirs for a few miles, I stopped for an hour at the Green Fence, known to me, where a woman with a double chin fries chicken the way my Aunt Margie did out in Ohio. Fritz does not fry chicken. At two o'clock I was rolling again, with only a couple of miles to go.

There was no point in phoning, since I was there anyway, but I almost had to, to find out where her cottage was. The cop on Main Street had never heard of Alice Porter. The man in the drugstore had, he had put up prescriptions for her, but didn't know where she lived. The man at the filling station thought her place was out toward Kent Cliffs but wasn't sure. He advised me to consult Jimmy Murphy, who ran a taxi. Jimmy rattled it off: a mile and a half west on Route 301, right on a blacktop for a mile, right on dirt for half a mile, mailbox on the right.

It checked. The half a mile of dirt was uphill, winding, narrow, and stony. The mailbox was at the mouth of a lane, even narrower, through a gap in a stone fence, no gate. I turned in and eased my way along the ruts to where the lane ended in front of a little house painted blue, one story. There was no car in sight. As I climbed out and shut the door a little bicolored mutt trotted up and started to growl, but his curiosity to see what I smelled like close up was too much for him, and the growl petered out. I reached down and scratched the back of his neck, and we were pals. He went with me to help knock on the door, and when, after knocking got no response, I tried the knob and found it was locked, he was as disappointed as I was.

With my years of training as a detective, I reached a conclusion. Dogs have to be fed. There was no other house in sight, no nearby neighbor to pinch-feed for Alice Porter. Therefore she would return. A top-drawer detective, say Nero Wolfe, could have found out exactly when she would return by looking at the dog's teeth and feeling its belly, but I'm not in that class. I looked over the grounds—four young trees and half a dozen shrubs scattered here and there—and then moseyed around to the back. There was a neat little vegetable garden, no weeds, and I pulled some radishes and ate them. Then I went to the car and got a book from my bag, I forget what, but it wasn't *The Moth That Ate Peanuts*, sat on one of two garden chairs in the shade of the house, and read. The mutt curled up at my feet and shut his eyes.

She came at 5:28. A '58 Ford station wagon came bumping along the ruts and stopped back of the Heron, and she scrambled out and headed for me. The mutt went bounding to meet her, and she halted to give him a pat. I shut my book and stood up.

"You looking for me?" she asked.

"I am if you're Miss Alice Porter," I said.

She knew who I was. It's easy to make a mistake on a thing like that, I had made plenty in my time, but it was in her eyes that she had recognized me or I had better quit the detective business and take up truck-driving or window-washing. That was nothing star-tling; it happened now and then. My picture hadn't been in the papers as often as President Eisenhower's, but it had once made the front page of the *Gazette*.

"That's my name," she said.

From her photograph I had guessed 150, but she had put on ten pounds. Her round face was bigger and her nose smaller, and her eyes were closer together. There was sweat on her brow.

"Mine's Archie Goodwin," I said. "I work for Nero Wolfe, the private detective. Could you give me maybe ten minutes?"

"I can if you'll wait till I put some stuff in the refrigerator. While I'm doing that you might get your car around back of mine. Take it easy on the grass."

I did so. The grass was nothing like that at 78 Haddon Place, but no doubt she would see to that after she collected from Amy Wynn. I moved the Heron forward a car length, cramped the wheels and backed, and swung around past the Ford and back into the ruts. She had got an armload of bags from the Ford, declining my offer to help, and entered the house. I returned to the chair, and soon she came out and took the other one.

"I've been thinking," she said. "If you're Archie Goodwin and Nero Wolfe sent you clear out here, it's not hard to guess what for. Or I should say who for. I might as well come right out with it. The Victory Press has hired him, or Amy Wynn has, to try to find something wrong about my claim for damages. If that's what it is you've wasted a lot of gas. I'm not going to talk about it, not a word. I may not be very bright, but I'm not exactly a fool. Unless you came to make an offer. I'll listen to that."

I shook my head. "That's not a very good guess, Miss Porter. It's about your claim against Amy Wynn, that much is okay, but she hasn't hired Mr. Wolfe and neither has the Victory Press. I'm here on behalf of a New York newspaper that's looking for a scoop. Nothing has been published about your claim, so I don't know how the paper got onto it, but you know how that is, word gets around. What the paper is after, it wants to publish your story, 'Opportunity Knocks,' on which you base your claim, with an introductory statement by you. It wants to know how much you will take for what it calls first serial rights, and it's not breaking any confidence to tell you that you can go pretty high. The reason they got Nero Wolfe to handle it instead of coming to you direct is that they want him to check on certain details. You understand that; it's sort of tricky."

"There's nothing tricky about my claim."

"I didn't say there is. But there would be a risk of a libel suit against the paper, whether there is ground for it or not. Of course before the paper makes a definite commitment it would want to see the story. Mr. Wolfe thought you might have a carbon copy and would let me take it. Have you got one?"

Her eyes met mine. They had been slanting off, first in one direction and then another, but now they came to me straight. "You're pretty good," she said.

"Thanks." I grinned at her. "I like to think so, but of course I'm biased. Good how?"

"Good with your tongue. I'll have to think it over. I'll do that. I'll think it over. Right now, as I said, I'm not going to talk about it. Not a word." She arose.

"But that was when you thought Mr. Wolfe had been hired by the Victory Press or Amy Wynn."

"I don't care who hired him, I'm not talking. You'll have to excuse me. I've got things to do." She headed for the door of the house. The mutt glanced at me and then at her, decided she was the best bet, and trotted after her. I went and got in the car and started the engine. On the stretch of blacktop a man with a bunch of wild columbine in his hand was following a herd of forty-seven cows (actual count; a detective is supposed to observe) who all had the same idea, that they would rather get hit by a Heron sedan than get milked, and it took me five minutes to get through.

Saturday afternoon at Lily Rowan's place, or it may have been Sunday afternoon, when half a dozen of us were loafing in the sun by the swimming pool, I told them about the incident on the terrace at Riverdale, leaving out the name and address and why I was there, and asked if they thought she was batty. The three women voted no and the two men yes, and of course that proved something but I still haven't decided what.

At midnight Sunday, full of air and with a sunburned nose, I dropped my bag in the hall of the old brownstone, went to the office, and found a note on my desk:

AG:
  Mr. Harvey phoned Saturday morning. He will come with his committee Monday at 11:15.
                                        NW

Chapter 6

This time there were seven instead of six. In addition to the three from the BPA—Gerald Knapp, Thomas Dexter, and Reuben Imhof—and the three from NAAD—Amy Wynn, Mortimer Oshin, and Philip Harvey—there was a middle-aged woman named Cora Ballard whose spine stayed as stiff as a poker both standing and sitting. Harvey had explained that she was not a committee member but was there ex officio. She was the executive secretary of the NAAD. Harvey had seen to it that she was seated next to him, at his left. I had noted glances directed at her by Dexter and Knapp which led me to suspect that in a national poll to choose the Secretary of the Year the book publishers' vote would not go to Cora Ballard, and her return glances indicated that she most certainly wouldn't want it to. She had a stenographer's notebook on her lap and a pencil in her hand.

Philip Harvey, in the red leather chair, was yawning, probably because he had had to get up and out before noon for the second time in a week. Gerald Knapp was explaining that he had been willing to cancel two appointments in order to be present because he agreed with Mr. Imhof that the charge now made by Alice Porter against Amy Wynn and the Victory Press made it imperative that immediate and vigorous action be taken, and he agreed with Mr. Harvey that they should see Mr. Wolfe in a body to learn what progress had been made. Wolfe, his lips pressed tight, sat and scowled at him.

"That is," Knapp finished, "if there has been any progress. Has there?"

"No," Wolfe said. "To the contrary. There has been regress."

They all stared. Cora Ballard said, "Really." Mortimer Oshin demanded, "How the hell could there be?"

Wolfe took a breath. "I'll explain briefly, and if you would like me to return the five thousand dollars you have advanced you have only to say so. I told you last Tuesday that this may be a laborious and costly operation; it now appears that it may take more labor than I am prepared to give, and cost more than you are prepared to pay. You were assuming that Alice Porter's success in hoodwinking Ellen Sturdevant had led others to imitate her, but you were wrong. Alice Porter was merely a tool, and so were Simon Jacobs, Jane Ogilvy, and Kenneth Rennert."

Cora Ballard looked up from her notebook. "Did you say 'tool'?"

"I did. Two steps brought me to that conclusion. The first resulted from my examination of the stories used by the three first-named as the bases of their claims. They were all written by the same person. The internal evidence—diction, syntax, paragraphing—is ineluctable. You are professional word-and-language people; study those stories and you'll all agree with me."

"I'm not a writer," Cora Ballard said. "I just work for writers."

"Not *for*," Harvey corrected her. "You work *with* writers and *on* writers." To Wolfe: "This is important, if true. I want to compare those stories."

"It's not only important," Knapp declared, "it's remarkable. It seems to me you *have* made progress."

"So it seemed to me," Wolfe said, "until I took the next step. All that remained, it seemed, was to learn which of the three had written the stories; then it would be simple. I procured a book written by Alice Porter, and one written by Simon Jacobs, and studied them, and I reread the testimony Jane Ogilvy had given on the witness stand, including the three poems she had recited. I shall not expound; I merely state that I am convinced that none of them wrote the stories."

"But damn it," Imhof objected, "somebody did! And now Alice Porter is repeating."

"By God," Oshin exclaimed, squashing a cigarette, "Rennert! Kenneth Rennert!"

Wolfe shook his head. "I doubt it. The reasons for my doubt are not conclusive, but they are cogent." He upturned a palm. "So. When you left here six days ago I thought I had four culprits to expose. When I had read the stories I thought I had just one and he could be easily identified; the others were only tools. That was progress. Now there is still just one, but who and where is he? The only approach to him, the only hope of finding him, is through the contacts he must have made with his tools. That kind of investigation does not fit my talents, and it will probably be prolonged and expensive. It will demand an exhaustive and meticulous inquiry into the movements and associations of those three people—four, with Kenneth Rennert included. That is regress."

"Do you mean you're quitting?" Dexter asked.

"I mean that it no longer seems to be my kind of job. To do it properly and with expedition at least a dozen competent operatives will be needed, with competent supervision. That will cost six hundred dollars a day or more, plus expenses, seven days a week. I would not supervise such an operation. But I should finish my report. As I told Mr. Harvey on the phone on Saturday, I sent Mr. Goodwin to call on those four people, and he has seen them. Archie?"

I had tossed my notebook over my shoulder onto my desk. It looked as if we weren't even going to send a bill for expenses, and in that case I was out $3.80 for the fried chicken I had bought at the Green Fence. "Do you want it all?" I asked.

"Not I. They. Miss Ballard is taking notes. If it isn't too extensive."

"It isn't. Two minutes with Simon Jacobs, seven with Kenneth Rennert, one with Jane Ogilvy, and eight with Alice Porter."

"Then verbatim."

I obliged. Since I had developed that faculty to a point where I could give Wolfe a full and accurate account of a two-hour conversation with three or four people, this little chore was nothing. As I went along I noticed that Mortimer Oshin was lighting no cigarettes, and I was taking it as a compliment until I realized that, being a dramatist, he was sizing up the dialogue. When I finished he reacted first.

"That Jane Ogilvy speech," he said. "Of course you've dressed it up. Damn good."

"No dressing," I told him. "When I report I merely report."

"And you think Kenneth Rennert is not the—the instigator?" Gerald Knapp asked.

"Right. For the reasons given."

"It seems to me," Philip Harvey said, "that this doesn't alter the situation any. As Mr. Wolfe described it." His head moved to take them in. "So now what?"

They held a committee meeting. What made it a meeting was that when more than three of them talked at once Harvey yelled that he couldn't hear anybody. After a quarter of an hour the consensus seemed to be that they were in a pickle, and I was thinking that if I were chairman I would ask for a motion to that effect.

Thomas Dexter raised his voice. "I would like to suggest," he suggested, "that we take twenty-four hours to consider the matter as it now stands, and meet again tomorrow. It is possible that Mr. Wolfe—"

"Wait a minute," Oshin cut in. He had a cigarette going. "I've got an idea." He stretched his neck to see around Gerald Knapp, to look at me. "A question for you, Mr. Goodwin. Which one of those four people needs money most?"

"That depends on what you mean by 'money,'" I told him. "A ten-spot or a grand or half a million?"

"Something in between. Here's my idea, and I like it. We make one of them an offer. Nero Wolfe makes it for us. Say ten thousand dollars. What the hell, I'd be willing to kick in that much myself. My lawyer thinks I may have to pay Rennert between fifty and a hundred thousand, and if this works Rennert will be done. And you're in the same position, Miss Wynn, with Alice Porter. She's going to nick you—"

"Not the same," Reuben Imhof objected. "There's no evidence. Alice Porter has claimed that Miss Wynn plagiarized a story she wrote, but the story hasn't been produced."

"It will be. Miss Wynn, wouldn't you be willing to pay ten thousand dollars to have Alice Porter stopped? Stopped for good?"

Amy Wynn looked at Imhof. He patted her on the shoulder. "Stopped how?" he asked Oshin. "What's your idea?"

"Very simple. Brilliant but simple. We offer him, or her, twenty thousand dollars to spill it. Who wrote the story he based his claim on, how the manuscript was planted—everything. With evidence to back it up; that should be easy. We also offer to guarantee that he won't be prosecuted and he won't be asked to return his share of the loot. You've seen all four of them, Mr. Goodwin. Which one would you pick?"

"Simon Jacobs," I said.

"Why him?"

"Very simple. Not even brilliant. Rennert is going to collect a lot more than twenty grand from you, or thinks he is. The same goes for Alice Porter; she has just made her claim on Amy Wynn. As for Jane Ogilvy, God only knows. She testified in court that she wrote that story, 'On Earth but Not in Heaven,' because she was suffocating under the blanket of her father's bounty and her mother's devotion and sought another market for her soul, end of quotation. I suppose meaning that she wanted to get hold of some cash, and presumably this operator knew that and obliged her. When she got it she kicked loose and went to Europe, but in a month she came back to the blanket. She might grab at the twenty grand, or she might spurn it. Just talking about her I use words like 'spurn.'"

"Then that leaves Jacobs."

"Right. He probably used up his share of the take

long ago. He's having a hard time placing his stories. He's living in a dump with his wife and children. I don't know if he's in debt, but he probably is, and he's not the kind of guy who would enjoy being in debt. He might open the bag for twenty grand if he had a tight guarantee that he wouldn't be prosecuted and he wouldn't be expected to repay what he got from Richard Echols more than two years ago. He hasn't got it any more. Of course the guarantee would have to come from Echols."

Oshin went to Thomas Dexter. "How about it, Mr. Dexter? You know Echols; you published his book. Of course I've met him, but I don't know him. Will he go along?"

The publisher passed his hand over his gray hair. "That's hard to say. I will say this, if Mr. Echols agrees to such an arrangement we at Title House will have no objection. We will concur, provided that Jacobs' affidavit—I presume it would be in the form of an affidavit—makes it clear that his charge of plagiarism was false. Provided it removes from Title House the stigma of having published a book that was—uh—a fraud. We would engage to make no demand for the return of our contribution to the payment made to Jacobs, or any part of it."

"That's fine. But what about Echols?"

"I couldn't say. He is a reasonable and sensible man in many respects. I think it quite possible that he would—uh—acquiesce, if properly approached."

"What do you think, Cora?" Philip Harvey asked. "You know him better than anyone here."

Cora Ballard pursed her lips. "Sure," she said, "I know Dick. I helped him with his first book contract twenty years ago, before he had an agent. The publisher wanted thirty per cent of the movie rights and twenty per cent of the first serial, and that was ridiculous. Dick's a little peculiar in some ways, but he likes to do the right thing and he's very generous. I'll ask him about this if you want me to, and see what he says. Actually, what he'll do, he'll go straight to Paul Norris, his agent, and ask him what he thinks. Of course I know Paul, and it might be better to take it up with him first. I could see him this afternoon."

"That's the kind of an executive secretary to have," Gerald Knapp said. "No wonder you authors always get the best of it."

Chairman Harvey snorted. "Comic relief. Always welcome. Speaking for myself, if I were Dick Echols I wouldn't hesitate. Unfortunately I'm not in his class and never will be. I've had six books published, and my last one, *Why the Gods Laugh*, is in its ninth thousand, which is a record for me." He looked around. "What about Mr. Oshin's idea? Do we like it?"

"I do," Oshin said. "Ten thousand dollars' worth, and I think Miss Wynn should match it."

Amy Wynn looked at Reuben Imhof. "We'll discuss it," he told her, and turned to the chairman. "It certainly won't do any harm for Miss Ballard to sound out Mr. Echols and his agent. If they agree to cooperate, then we can decide whether to go ahead."

"In my opinion," Gerald Knapp said, "we should decide that now. I fully approve of Mr. Oshin's suggestion and move that we adopt it. If Mr. Echols consents it shouldn't be necessary to have another meeting. Mr. Wolfe could proceed at once to have the necessary papers drawn and make the offer to Simon Jacobs."

"Second the motion," Oshin said.

"Further discussion?" Harvey asked. "If not, all in favor raise your hands. It seems to be unanimous. Miss

Wynn, when can you let me know whether you will match Mr. Oshin's ten thousand? Today?"

"Oh, yes," she assured him. "Certainly by five o'clock."

"Good. If I'm not at home call Miss Ballard at the NAAD. Now, Mr. Wolfe, I hope this has changed your mind. I hope you'll agree that we're making some progress, and of course you and Mr. Goodwin made it possible. Have you any comment?"

"Yes," Wolfe said. "I am a detective, not a conveyor of bait. However, since Mr. Goodwin named Mr. Jacobs as the prospective receiver, he and I have a responsibility. If the preparations are satisfactory, we will act."

Chapter 7

At twenty minutes past four that afternoon Amy Wynn told me, not on the phone, in person, that she would match Oshin's ten grand.

The development started shortly after three o'clock with a phone call from Reuben Imhof. Wolfe and I were in the office, having lunched together in the dining room in a slightly improved atmosphere. He was at his desk dictating letters, and I was at mine taking them, when the phone rang and I answered it.

"Nero Wolfe's office, Archie Goodwin speaking."

"This is Reuben Imhof. I understand that Wolfe never leaves his house on business."

"Correct. He doesn't."

"All right, you, then. Come up here quick. My office, Victory Press."

"I'm pretty busy. Say in an hour?"

"No. Now. Nothing I can tell you on the phone. *Now!*"

"Okay. Coming. Keep your shirt on." I hung up and told Wolfe, "Imhof. Something is biting him, he wouldn't say what, and he wants me quick. Our responsibility?"

Wolfe grunted. "Confound these interruptions." We

were in the middle of a letter to Lewis Hewitt, describing the results of a cross of *C. gaskelliana alba* with *C. mossiae wageneri.* "Very well. Go."

I did so. At that time of day taxis are apt to crawl slightly faster on Eighth Avenue than on Tenth, so I headed east. We finally made it to 52nd and Sixth Avenue, and when we turned right and I saw that the whole block was choked I paid the hackie and quit him. The Victory Press address, on Madison in the Fifties, was one of the new concrete and glass boxes, with a green marble lobby and four banks of elevators. As I entered the suite on the thirty-second floor I half expected to find the place in an uproar, from the way Imhof had sounded on the phone, but all was serene. The two people on chairs in the reception room, one of them with a bulging briefcase on his lap, merely looked patient, and the bright-eyed receptionist at the desk merely lifted her brows as I approached. However, when I told her my name she said Mr. Imhof was expecting me and used the phone, and in a moment an attractive young woman entered through an arch and asked me to follow her, please; and being, as I have said, a trained observer, naturally I noticed that she had restless hips.

Reuben Imhof's room was an ideal setting for discussing the terms of a book contract with a member of the NAAD. Surely an author wouldn't be fussy about little things with a man who had a desk like that, and such fine comfortable chairs, and four windows on two sides, and genuine oil paintings on the walls, and real old Persian rugs. Having taken that in with a quick glance around, I crossed to the desk. Imhof, behind it, kept his seat and his hands. From his look he was in no mood to shake hands with William Shakespeare or Mark Twain if one of them had suddenly entered. He didn't greet me at all. Instead, he spoke to the young woman who had ushered me in. "Don't go, Judith. Sit down. Look at this, Goodwin."

I didn't hop. It may be true that, as a friend once told me, I have no more social grace than a conceited tiger, but Amy Wynn, being a member of the committee, was one-sixth of our client and not to be ignored. So before looking at the object Imhof had on his desk I turned to the chair where Amy Wynn was sitting and told her good afternoon. She nodded, just barely. Then I looked at the object.

It was some sheets of paper, 8½ by 11. The one on top was headed "Opportunity Knocks," and below that, "by Alice Porter." In the upper right-hand corner was a date, June 3, 1957. The text that followed was double-spaced. I lifted the edges to the last sheet: twenty-seven pages. There were no creases from folding.

"By God," Imhof said.

"I doubt it," I said. "I doubt if He had a hand in it. Probably not by Alice Porter, either. Where was it?"

"In a cabinet in the filing room down the hall. In a folder marked 'Amy Wynn.'"

"Who found it?"

"Miss Frey, my secretary." He aimed a thumb at the attractive young woman. "Miss Judith Frey."

"When?"

"About ten minutes before I phoned you. Miss Wynn was here with me. We were discussing the contents of a letter I wrote her last week, and I sent for Miss Frey and asked her to bring the carbon. She brought the whole folder, because, she said, of something that was in it. The 'something' was that. She says it wasn't in the folder last Wednesday, five days ago, the last time she had occasion to go to it. I want to ask you something. Do you remember that this morning Mortimer Oshin said Miss Wynn was in the same position with Alice Porter as he was with Kenneth Rennert, and I said it wasn't the same because the story hadn't been produced, and he said, 'It will be'? Not 'It may be,' 'It will be.' Remember that?"

"Nuts." I moved a chair around and sat. "People say things. How much have you handled it?"

"Not much. I glanced through it. So did Miss Wynn."

"It probably doesn't matter. Whoever put it there has probably heard of fingerprints. Who has access to that room?"

"Everybody here."

"How many?"

"In this department, executive and editorial, thirty-two. Altogether, more than a hundred, but people in other departments never go to that room."

"But they could?"

"Yes."

"Is there always somebody in that room? Someone stationed there?"

"No one is stationed there, but people are always going and coming."

"Then an outsider could just walk in?"

"I suppose he could." Imhof leaned forward. "Look, Goodwin. I got you here immediately. This is hot. Nero Wolfe is supposed to be the best there is, or you and he together are. We want you to get this sonofabitch, and get him quick. Miss Wynn wants you to, and so do I."

"Him or her."

"Okay. But quick. By God!" He hit the desk with his fist. "Planting it here in this office! What are you going to do? What do you want me to do?"

I crossed my legs. "It's a little complicated. Mr.

Wolfe already has a client, the Joint Committee on Plagiarism, of which you and Miss Wynn are members. There could be a conflict of interest. For instance, considering this case alone, independently, possibly the best course would be to forget that this thing was found. Burn it or let me stash it. But the committee wouldn't like that because it may be helpful in stopping this plagiarism racket for good, which is what they want. How many people know this thing has been found?"

"Three. Miss Wynn, Miss Frey, and I. And you. Four."

"How long has Miss Frey been with you?"

"About a year."

"Then you don't know her very well."

"I know her well enough. She was recommended by my former secretary when she left to get married."

I looked at Judith Frey and back at Imhof. "There are two obvious questions about her. One, did she put that thing in the folder herself? Two, granting that she didn't, could she be trusted to forget that she found it if you asked her to? If not, it would be very risky—"

"I didn't, Mr. Goodwin." Miss Frey had a clear, strong voice. "I can see why you ask that, but I didn't. And if my employer asked me to do anything I couldn't be trusted to do, I would quit."

"Good for you." I returned to Imhof. "But actually I'm just talking. Even if you decide you can trust Miss Frey to keep her mouth shut and burn that thing, what about me? I have seen it. I will of course report to Mr. Wolfe, and he will act in the interest of his client, the committee, and you may find—"

"We're not going to burn it," Amy Wynn blurted. Her nose was twitching. Her eyes were red. Her hands, in her lap, were fists. She went on, "I never saw that thing before, and nobody can prove I did! I hate this! I *hate* it!"

I moved to her. "Naturally you do, Miss Wynn. And after all, you're the one that will get soaked if Alice Porter gets away with it. Would you like to know what I would advise you to do?"

"I certainly would."

"This is just off the cuff. After I report to Mr. Wolfe he may change it. First, let me take that manuscript. I'll try it for fingerprints, but that's probably hopeless. Mr. Wolfe will compare it with the others. Second, say nothing about it to anyone. You have no lawyer?"

"No."

"Okay. Third, don't communicate with Alice Porter. If you get a letter from her, don't answer it. If she calls you on the phone, hang up. Fourth, let Mr. Wolfe handle this as a part of what he has already been hired for. He can't question everyone who works here himself, or anyhow he won't, but he has a couple of good men who will do it for him—provided Mr. Imhof will cooperate."

"Cooperate hell," Imhof said. "I'm in this as much as she is. Are you through?"

"No." I stayed with Amy Wynn. "Fifth and last, I think there's at least an even chance that Mortimer Oshin's idea will work. From the look on Simon Jacobs' face when I asked him if he would do an article on how it felt to have his story stolen, I think he's hating himself. I think he did it because he was hard up and had a family and had to have cash, and he wishes he hadn't and would be glad to get it off his chest, and if he can spit it out without fear of going to jail, and get paid besides, I think he will. That's only what I think, but I saw his face. If I'm right this whole thing will be cracked wide open. And the bait ought to be as juicy as possible, and twenty thousand is twice as juicy as ten. So fifth, I strongly advise you to tell me now that we can make it twenty."

Her nose twitched. "You mean I agree to pay ten thousand dollars."

"Right. Provided Richard Echols does his part."

She looked at Imhof. "Should I?"

Imhof spoke to me. "That's what we were discussing earlier. We hadn't decided. I was inclined to be against it. But now, by God, I'm for it. I'm for it so much that I'll commit Victory Press right now to pay half of it. Five thousand. And five thousand from you, Amy?"

"Yes," she said. "Thank you, Reuben."

"Don't thank me. Thank the bastard that planted that thing here in my office. Do you want it in writing?"

"No." I stood up. "I'll go and see if Mr. Wolfe approves the advice I gave you. You'll be hearing from him. I need some sheets of glossy paper and a stamp pad. For sets of prints of you three so I can eliminate them. And some large envelopes."

That took some time, getting three sets of legible prints with an ordinary stamp pad, and it was nearly five o'clock when I got away, with Imhof doing me the honor of escorting me to the elevator. I decided to walk it. It would take only a few minutes more than a creeping taxi, and my legs needed stretching. After mounting the stoop and letting myself in, I stepped to the end of the hall to stick my head in the kitchen and let Fritz know I was back, and then went to the office, put the envelopes on my desk, and got brushes and powder and other items from a drawer of a cabinet. I couldn't qualify as a fingerprint expert in a courtroom, but for private purposes I will do.

When Wolfe came down from the plant rooms at six o'clock he started for his desk, saw the clutter on mine, stopped, and demanded, "What have you got there?"

I swiveled. "Very interesting. I've done the first nine pages of this manuscript, 'Opportunity Knocks,' by Alice Porter, and there's no sign of a print, let alone an identifiable one, except Amy Wynn's and Miss Frey's and Imhof's. That justifies the assumption that it was either carefully wiped or was only handled with gloves on. In that case—"

"Where did you get it?" He was at my elbow, surveying the clutter.

I told him, including the dialogue. When I got to where Imhof had said there were thirty-two people in the executive and editorial departments of Victory Press, he went to his desk and sat. At the end I said, "If you want to make any changes in the advice I gave her, I have her home phone number. As I told her, it was off the cuff and subject to your approval."

He grunted. "Satisfactory. You realize, of course, that this may be merely an added complication, not an advance."

"Sure. Some person unknown somehow got a key to that office and sneaked in after hours and put it in Amy Wynn's folder. As before, possibly, in Ellen Sturdevant's bureau drawer and Marjorie Lippin's trunk. The only difference is that this is hot—as Imhof said."

"It's recent," he conceded. "Give me the nine pages you have finished with."

I took them to him and returned to my desk and started on page ten. Fritz, responding to a summons, brought beer, and Wolfe opened the bottle and poured.

Page ten had nothing. Page eleven had only two useless smudges, one on the front and one on the back, near a corner. Page twelve had a fair right thumb and a poor right index finger of Reuben Imhof. I was on page thirteen when Wolfe's voice came. "Give me the rest of it."

"I've only done three more pages. I want—"

"I want all of it. I'll take care."

I took it to him, taking care, and then went to the kitchen to see how Fritz was getting on with the braised duckling stuffed with crabmeat, because I didn't want to sit and watch Wolfe smearing up the last fifteen pages. It isn't that he doesn't believe in fingerprints; it's just that they are only routine and therefore a genius can't be expected to bother about them. However, by going to the kitchen I merely transferred from one genius to another. When I offered to spread the paste on the cheesecloth which was to be wrapped around the ducklings, Fritz gave me exactly the kind of look Wolfe has given me on various and numerous occasions. I was perched on a stool, making pointed comments to Fritz about the superiority of teamwork, when there was a bellow from the office.

"Archie!"

I went. Wolfe was leaning back with his palms on the chair arms. "Yes, sir?"

"This *is* a complication. It was written by Alice Porter."

"Sure. It says so at the top."

"Don't be flippant. You fully expected, and so did I, to find that it had been written by the same person as the other three. It wasn't. Pfui!"

"Well, well, as Kenneth Rennert would say. Of course you're sure?"

"Certainly."

"And also sure that Alice Porter did write it?"

"Yes."

I went to my chair and sat. "Then she decided to do one on her own, that's all. Obviously. That doesn't help any, but it doesn't hinder either. Does it?"

"It may. It makes it extremely likely that the one we're after, the one we must find and expose, had no hand in this, and therefore we should waste no time or effort on it. Miss Wynn is not our client, and neither is Mr. Imhof. They are merely members of that committee. Of immediate concern is the fact that they were under a misapprehension when they agreed to contribute ten thousand dollars to the bait for Simon Jacobs. They assumed that this is another operation by the same person, and it isn't. We must tell them so, and when we do they will probably decline to make the contribution."

"Yeah." I scratched my nose. I scratched my cheek. "Yeah. So they will. You work too hard. You read too much. I don't suppose you could forget you read the damn thing? Just forget it for twenty-four hours, say?"

"No, and neither could you. You'll have to phone them at once. Is it out of the question to offer Simon Jacobs as little as ten thousand?"

I shook my head. "No, not out of the question. I'd start at ten anyhow, but I'd like it better if I knew I could boost it. He might even take five. I could start at five."

"Very well. Call Miss Wynn. I'll speak with her."

I swiveled, but as I reached for the phone it rang. It was Philip Harvey. He asked for Wolfe, and Wolfe took his receiver. I stayed on.

"Yes, Mr. Harvey? This is Nero Wolfe."

"I have good news, Mr. Wolfe. Thanks to Cora Bal-

lard. She has it all fixed with Richard Echols. She saw
Paul Norris, his agent, and she saw him, and I've just
had a talk with Echols, and it's all set. Dexter's lawyer
will draw the necessary papers in the morning, one for
Echols to sign and one for Title House, and they'll be
ready by noon. I've spoken with Mortimer Oshin, and
he wants to know whether you want the ten thousand
in cash or a certified check."

"Cash would be better, I think."

"All right, I'll tell him. What about Amy Wynn? Is
she coming across?"

"It's uncertain. There has been a development. The
manuscript of the story on which Alice Porter bases
her claim was found this afternoon in a file in the office
of the Victory Press."

"*No!* I'll be damned! In Imhof's office? Wonderful!
Marvelous! Then of course she will. She'll have to."

"She may. There are complexities, now unresolved,
which I'll report on later. In any case, it will probably
be best to give Jacobs only half of the agreed amount
now, and the other half later, contingent on his satisfactory cooperation. If Miss Wynn won't supply it,
someone will. Your committee will see to that."

"I suppose so. I can't promise it."

"I don't ask you to. I will engage to put it up to Mr.
Knapp, Mr. Dexter, and Mr. Imhof. They couldn't possibly wriggle out of it."

"Ha! You don't know how publishers can wriggle.
They're experts. They're champions."

"That will make it all the more satisfying to pin
them. Satisfying both to you and to me—if it proves to
be necessary. Ten thousand may be enough. I will be
responsible for any commitments I make."

Wolfe hung up and turned to me. "Get Miss Wynn."

Chapter 8

At half past five the next day, Tuesday, I entered the vestibule of the tenement at 632 West 21st Street and pressed the button by Simon Jacobs' name. In my breast pocket were two documents, one signed by Richard Echols and the other signed by Thomas Dexter for Title House. Both were notarized. In my side pocket was a neat little package containing five thousand dollars in twenties, fifties, and Cs. Another five thousand was distributed among other pockets, not in packages.

I could have been there two hours earlier but for the fact that no hurricane had hit town. Nothing less than a hurricane would make Wolfe cancel his afternoon session in the plant rooms, from four to six, and it had been decided that instead of trying to hook Jacobs myself I was to bring him to 35th Street and watch Wolfe do it, chiefly because it would be desirable to have a witness. I was not to be visible; I would be stationed in the alcove at the end of the hall with my notebook, at the hole in the wall, concealed by a trick picture on the office side, through which I could both see and hear. I had the documents and money with me because it might take more than words to get Jacobs to come.

There had been no snags. Shortly after twelve Cora Ballard, the executive secretary of NAAD, had come in person with the documents. She had brought them instead of sending them because she wanted to brief us on Simon Jacobs, whom she had known for nearly thirty years, ever since he had joined NAAD in 1931. He had always been a little odd, but she had always regarded him as honest and honorable, so much so that when he had accused Richard Echols of plagiarism she had had a faint suspicion that there might be something to it, but had abandoned it when she tried to get in touch with him and he wouldn't talk. He was proud and touchy and he loved his wife and kids, and her advice was not to threaten him or try to get tough with him but just show him the money and the documents and put it on a basis of common sense. All of which might have been very helpful if it hadn't been for the fact that he had already been dead about fourteen hours.

No, no snags. It couldn't be called a snag that Amy Wynn and Reuben Imhof had withdrawn their offer to sweeten the pot, since that had been expected. While Wolfe and I were at lunch a messenger had arrived with the ten thousand dollars' worth of lettuce from Mortimer Oshin.

So at five-thirty I pressed the button in the vestibule, the click came, and I opened the door and entered. I was ready for the garlic and took a deep breath as I headed for the stairs. My opening line was on my tongue. Three flights up I turned to the front, and there, at the open door where Mrs. Jacobs and the boy had awaited me on my previous visit, I was again awaited, but not by them. In the dim light I took two steps before I recognized him, then stopped. We spoke simultaneously, and spoke the same words.

"Not *you*," we said.

I knew. As Jane Ogilvy would have put it, a fact felt though not perceived. The presence there of Sergeant Purley Stebbins of Homicide West might have meant any one of a dozen things—one of the kids had been killed by a hit-and-run driver, or Jacobs had killed his wife, or one of them was merely being questioned about some other death by violence—but I knew. It had to be. That was why I said, "Not *you*."

"I've been here five minutes," Purley said. "Just five minutes, and here *you* come. Jumping Jesus!"

"I've only been here five seconds," I said, "and here *you* are. I came to see a man named Simon Jacobs on business. Please tell him I'm here."

"What kind of business?"

"A private kind."

His jaw worked. "Look, Goodwin." He has been known to call me Archie, but in different circumstances. "I come here on a job. If I'm somewhere on a job and someone asks me who is the last person on God's earth I would want to show up, I would name you. What I'd like, I'd like to tell you to go somewhere and scratch your ass with your elbow. A man's body is found. He was murdered. We get him identified. I go to where he lived to ask some questions, and I no sooner get started than the bell rings and I go to the door, and it's you, and you say you came to see him on business. When you come to see a corpse on business, I know what to expect. I'm asking you, what kind of business?"

"I told you. Private and personal."

"When did you learn Jacobs had been killed? And how? He was identified only an hour ago."

"Just now. From you." I had joined him at the door. "Let's take a short cut, Sergeant. The long way would be for you to bark at me a while, getting upset because I won't unload, and then you would take me to Homicide West, only a short walk, which you have no right to do, so *I* would get upset, and then Inspector Cramer would go to see Mr. Wolfe, and so on. The short way would be for me to phone Mr. Wolfe and get his permission to tell you why I came to see Jacobs, which he would probably give because there's no reason why he shouldn't and it may be connected with his death. You know damn well that without his permission I tell you nothing."

"You admit it's connected."

"Nuts. You're not the DA and we're not in court. Of course Mr. Wolfe will want some details—when and how he was killed, and by whom, if you know."

Purley opened his mouth and shut it again. When I have facts he needs, he would like to force them out by jumping up and down on my belly, but for that I would have to be lying on my back.

"With me listening," he said.

"Sure, why not?"

"Okay. The body was found at two o'clock this afternoon behind a bush in Van Cortlandt Park. It had been dragged across the grass from the edge of the road, so it was probably taken there in a car. There was one stab wound in the chest with a broad blade. No weapon found. The ME says between nine o'clock and midnight. Probably nothing taken. Eighteen dollars in his wallet. You can call Wolfe on the phone in here."

"Any leads?"

"No."

"When or where he went last night, or who with?"

"No. I was asking his wife when you came. She says she doesn't know. The phone's in his room, where he worked. Where he wrote. He wrote stories."

"I know he did. What time did he go out?"

"Around eight o'clock. If he had an appointment he made it on the phone and she didn't know anything about it. So she says. I just got started with her. I brought her here from the morgue after she identified the body. She says he told her he was going to see somebody and might be late, and that was all. If Wolfe wants to know what he had in his stomach he'll have to wait until—"

"Don't be flippant. Where's the phone?"

We went inside and he shut the door and led the way down the narrow hall to a door on the left. It was a small room with one window, a table with a typewriter, shelves with books and magazines, and a row of drawers. There were two chairs, and on one of them was Mrs. Jacobs. I said she wasn't a crone when I saw her five days before, but she was now. I wouldn't have known her. As we entered her eyes came to us. She focused on me, staring, and blurted, "It was you!"

"What?" Purley asked her. "Do you know this man?"

"I've seen him." She was on her feet. "He was here last week. His name's Goodwin. My husband saw him just for a minute, and after he left Simon told me if he ever came again to shut the door on him." She was trembling all over. "I knew from the way—"

"Take it easy, Mrs. Jacobs." Purley had her arm. "I know this Goodwin. I'll handle him, don't worry. You can tell me about it later." He was easing her out. "You go and lie down a while. Drink something. Drink some hot tea. . . ."

He got her to the hall. In a moment he returned,

shut the door, and turned. "So you've been here before."

"Sure. With Mr. Wolfe's permission I'll confess everything."

"There's the phone."

I sat at the table and dialed, and after five rings had Fritz, who always answers when Wolfe is up with the orchids. I told him to buzz the plant rooms, and after a wait Wolfe's voice came. "Yes?"

"I have to report another complication. I'm in Simon Jacobs' apartment, the room he wrote stories in. Sergeant Stebbins is with me. He is investigating the murder of Simon Jacobs, whose body was found at two o'clock this afternoon behind a bush in Van Cortlandt Park. Stabbed. Between nine and twelve last night. Body taken there in a car. No leads. No anything."

"Confound it!"

"Yes, sir. Stebbins was here when I arrived, and naturally he is curious. Are there any details I should save?"

Silence. Ten seconds, then: "No. There's nothing worth saving."

"Right. Tell Fritz to save some of that shashlik for me. I'll be home when I get there." I hung up and told Purley, "He says there's nothing worth saving. Shall I just tell it or would you rather grill me?"

"Try telling it," he said, and got the chair the widow had vacated, sat, and got out his notebook.

Chapter 9

Thomas Dexter of Title House squared his shoulders and set his long, bony jaw. "I don't care how you look at it, Mr. Harvey," he said. "I know how *I* look at it. I'm not condemning Mr. Wolfe or the members of this committee, or even myself, but I have a feeling of guilt. I regard myself as guilty of incitation to murder. Unwittingly, yes, but what are wits for? I should have considered the possible consequences of signing that agreement not to prosecute Simon Jacobs."

It was noon the next day, Wednesday. If you are fed up with committee meetings, so was Wolfe and so was I, but that's one disadvantage of having a committee for a client. And it was no longer merely a Joint Committee on Plagiarism. Within two hours after I had supplied the details to Stebbins they had all been visited by city employees. Knapp had been interrupted in the middle of a bridge game. Oshin had been found at dinner at Sardi's. Imhof and Amy Wynn had been called from a conference with three other executives of Victory Press. Dexter and Harvey and Cora Ballard had received the callers at home. Harvey had elicited these details from them so Wolfe would realize the gravity of the situation.

Having come at eleven o'clock, they had been at it for an hour, and there had been raised voices and heated words, with no unanimity on anything. Take the question, did they accept the assumption that Jacobs had been killed to keep him from squealing? Knapp and Harvey said no, he might have been killed from some quite different motive; it might have been merely coincidence. Dexter and Oshin said yes, that they couldn't get from under a responsibility by laying it to coincidence. Imhof and Amy Wynn and Cora Ballard were on the fence. Wolfe ended that argument by saying that it didn't matter whether they accepted the assumption or not; the police had made it, and so had he, as a working hypothesis.

Of course that led to a hotter question. If Jacobs had been killed to keep him from telling who had written "What's Mine Is Yours" and got him to make his claim on Richard Echols, the murderer must have known about the plan to pry Jacobs open. Who had told him? That was what the cops had been after when they called on the members of the committee, and that was what Wolfe wanted, but look what they got:

Amy Wynn had told two friends, a man and a woman, with whom she had dined Monday evening. Cora Ballard had told the president and vice-president of NAAD and two members of its council. Mortimer Oshin had told his lawyer, his agent, his producer, and his wife. Gerald Knapp had told his lawyer and two members of his firm. Reuben Imhof had told three of his associates at Victory Press. Philip Harvey had told no one, he said. Thomas Dexter had told his secretary, his lawyer, and six members of the board of directors of Title House. So, counting the committee members and Wolfe and me, thirty-three people had known about it. Supposing they had passed it on to others as an interesting inside item, averaging one apiece, which wasn't hard to suppose, that would make a total of sixty-six. And supposing . . . You do it.

Hopeless.

Another question: what was the committee going to do now? In Gerald Knapp's opinion, it should do nothing. It should await events. Since the police were assuming that the murderer had been motivated by the urgent necessity to silence Jacobs, they would concentrate on the effort to learn who had written the stories and instigated the claims, and, though that would have its disagreeable aspects, it meant that the purpose for which the committee was formed was now being served by the vast resources of the New York police, and in comparison the resources of the committee were nothing. Philip Harvey agreed, possibly because for the third time in nine days he had had to be up and out before noon and he wanted to catch up on his sleep. Amy Wynn supposed it wouldn't hurt to wait and see what the police did. Cora Ballard thought there should be a special meeting of the NAAD council to consider the matter, that the council had authorized the committee to deal with plagiarism claims, not with murder.

But Thomas Dexter and Mortimer Oshin couldn't see it, and neither could Reuben Imhof. They were all emphatic that Wolfe should be told to go ahead, though for different reasons. Imhof's point was that there was no telling how long it would take the police to find the plagiarist, if they ever did, and their messing around and the publicity would be bad for both publishers and authors. Oshin's point was more personal. He had put up ten thousand dollars in cash in the hope that it would help to stop Kenneth Rennert, and he wanted Wolfe to go ahead and use it for that purpose, with or without the concurrence of the committee. Thomas Dexter's point was even more personal, as you saw from the speech he made to Harvey. He regarded himself as guilty of incitation to murder. Apparently he had an old-fashioned conscience. He went on to say that he couldn't shift his responsibility to the police, he wanted Wolfe to go ahead and spare no pains or expense, and he would contribute any sum that might be required. He didn't even say "within reason."

He ended by making a motion, and the chairman asked for hands. Three went up at once—Dexter's, Imhof's, and Oshin's. Then Amy Wynn's, not with enthusiasm. Cora Ballard remarked that she wasn't a committee member and couldn't vote. Gerald Knapp asked her to record him as voting nay.

"Even if the chairman could vote," Harvey said, "it would be four to two." He turned to Wolfe. "So you go ahead. The last time you went ahead you got a man killed. What next?"

"That's pretty raw," Oshin said. "It was my idea, and the vote was unanimous."

Harvey ignored him. He repeated to Wolfe, "What next?"

Wolfe cleared his throat. "I am twice a jackass," he said.

They stared. He nodded. "First, I should never have accepted a committee as a client. That was egregious. Second, I should not have consented to act as a mere conveyor of bait. That was fatuous. It dulled my faculties. Having become a party to a procedure which made an obvious target of a man, which put a man in imminent danger, and aware that all of you knew of it and others soon would, I was an ass not to take precautions. I should have seen to it that he was not harmed. It was even quite possible that one of you was the wretch I had engaged to expose."

"Sure," Harvey said. "Now you're getting hot."

"It could be you, Mr. Harvey. With your most successful book only in its ninth thousand, you must have been open to temptation. So while I do not have Mr. Dexter's feeling of guilt, that I incited to murder, I do strongly feel that I failed to function properly. But for my default Mr. Jacobs would be alive, and probably we would have our man. It was understood that you may terminate your engagement with me at will. I invite you to do so now."

Three of them said no—Oshin, Imhof, and Dexter. The others said nothing. Wolfe asked the chairman, "Do you want a vote on it, Mr. Harvey?"

"No," Harvey said. "It would be four to one again."

"It would be unanimous," Gerald Knapp said. "I did not suggest that we should terminate the engagement."

Wolfe grunted. "Very well. I should tell you that if you do terminate it, I shall not withdraw. I have a score to settle—with myself. I have bruised my self-esteem and I intend to heal it. I am going to expose the murderer of Simon Jacobs, anticipating the police if possible, and presumably that will also solve your problem. I shall do that in any case, but if I act as your agent it must be with a free hand. I won't tell you what I intend to do. If one of you makes a suggestion other than privately, as Mr. Oshin did, I'll reject it without reference to its merits. Since I can't rely on your discretion, you will have to rely on mine."

"That's a lot to ask," Knapp said.

"No, sir. It is asking nothing; it is merely notifying you. If I told you I intended to do something and then did something else, I would still be your agent. You must trust my probity and my judgment in any case, or dismiss me."

"What the hell," Oshin said. "You've got my ten thousand, go ahead and use it." He looked at his watch and stood up. "I'm late for an appointment."

The meeting adjourned at 12:48 p.m. without a motion. Thomas Dexter stayed for a word with Wolfe, not to make a private suggestion but to repeat that he felt a personal responsibility and would personally contribute any necessary amount. This time, however, he added "within reason." It's fine to have a conscience, but you can't just let it run wild.

When Dexter had gone, Wolfe leaned back and closed his eyes. I put the extra chairs back in place, treated myself to a good stretch, went to the kitchen and drank a glass of water, and returned. I stood and looked down at him.

"I was wondering," I said. "Am I included in that?"

"In what?" he asked without opening his eyes.

"In the lockout. I won't be much help if you refuse to tell me what you intend to do."

"Pfui."

"I'm glad to hear it. I would like to say that I have a little self-esteem too, of course not in the same class as yours, and it needs attention. Yesterday Purley Stebbins asked me, and I quote, 'Why the hell did you set the guy up like that and then come here today and expect to find him whole?' That was the first time a Homicide man has ever asked me a question I couldn't answer. If I had told him because you were a jackass and so was I, he would have wanted to include it in my signed statement."

He grunted. He hadn't opened his eyes.

"So we're to go ahead," I said. "Lunch is about

ready, and business is out at the table, and you like to
rest your brain during digestion, so you might give me
instructions now. Where do we start?"

"I have no idea."

"It might be a good plan to get one, since you intend to anticipate the police. I suppose I could call on
the committee members separately and ask for suggestions—"

"Shut up."

So we were back to normal.

When Wolfe went up to the plant rooms at four
o'clock I still had no instructions, but I wasn't biting
nails. During the hour and a half since lunch he had
picked up his current book four times, read a paragraph, and put it down again; he had turned on the
television three times and turned it off; he had counted
the bottle caps in his desk drawer twice; and he had
got up and walked over to the big globe and spent ten
minutes studying geography. So, since he was hard at
work, there was no point in needling him.

I passed the time—an hour of it in comparing the
typewriting of "Opportunity Knocks," by Alice Porter,
with "There Is Only Love," also by Alice Porter, and
"What's Mine Is Yours," by Simon Jacobs. No two on
the same machine. I reread the carbon of the statement I had given Purley Stebbins, found nothing that
needed correcting, and filed it. I reread the piece in the
morning *Times* about the murder, and when the *Gazette* came, around five-thirty, I read that. The *Times*
had no mention of plagiarism or the NAAD or the
BPA. The *Gazette* had a paragraph about the plagiarism charge Jacobs had made against Richard Echols
in 1956, but there was no hint that his death had any
connection with it. I was wondering why Lon Cohen
hadn't called when the phone rang and there he was.

He stated his case: I had phoned him nine days ago to ask him about the NAAD and the BPA. Simon Jacobs, murdered Monday night, was a member of NAAD. Tuesday evening I had arrived at Homicide West on 20th Street with Sergeant Stebbins, who was working on the Jacobs case, and had stayed four hours. Would I therefore please tell him immediately why I had inquired about the NAAD, who was Wolfe's client, and who had killed Jacobs and why, with all relevant details which the public had a right to know. I told him I would call him back as soon as I had anything fit to print, probably in a couple of months, and said I would be glad to send him a glossy of a photograph I had just taken, which the public had a right to see.

There was another phone call, from Cora Ballard, the executive secretary. She said she had been worrying about the decision of the committee to let Nero Wolfe go ahead with a free hand. She appreciated the fact that a private detective couldn't very well tell a group of people what he was doing and going to do, but the committee had no authority to hire a detective to investigate a murder, and naturally she was worried. It wouldn't be easy to get a large attendance of the NAAD council on short notice, but she could probably set one up for Monday or Tuesday of next week, and would I ask Mr. Wolfe to take no important steps until then? She was afraid that if he went ahead and did something drastic he would be acting without authority, and she thought he ought to know that. I told her I thought so too and I would certainly tell him. There's no point in being rude when you can end a conversation quicker by being polite.

I had the radio on for the six-o'clock news when Wolfe came down from the plant rooms. He had a cluster of Phalaenopsis Aphrodite in his hand, and he got a vase from the shelf, took it to the kitchen for water, brought it back, put the stem in, and placed it on his desk. That's the only hard work he ever does around the office. When the news stopped for a commercial I turned it off and told him, "Still nothing about plagiarism or our clients or you. If the cops have made any headway they're playing it close—"

The doorbell rang, and I stepped to the hall for a look through the one-way glass panel. A glance was enough. I turned to tell Wolfe, "Cramer."

He made a face. "Alone?"

"Yes."

He took a breath. "Let him in."

Chapter 10

Inspector Cramer of Homicide West had sat in the red leather chair facing the end of Wolfe's desk oftener and longer than any other three people combined. He just about filled it. How he sat depended on circumstances. I have seen him leaning back with his legs crossed, comfortable and relaxed, with a glass of beer in his hand. I have also seen him with his broad rump just catching the edge, his jaw set and his lips tight, his big red face three shades redder, his gray eyes bulging.

That day he was in between, at least at the start. He declined Wolfe's offer of beer, but he made himself comfortable. He said he'd just stopped in on his way somewhere, which meant he wanted something he knew damn well a phone call wouldn't get. Wolfe said it was pleasant to see him, which meant "What do you want?" Cramer took a cigar from his pocket, which meant that he expected it to take more than a couple of minutes to get what he was after.

"This Jacobs thing is a hash if I ever saw one," Cramer said.

Wolfe nodded. "It is indeed."

"One thing about it, I've heard something I never

heard before. I've heard Sergeant Stebbins pay you and Goodwin a compliment. He says as smart as you are, you couldn't possibly have arranged that scheme to buy Jacobs, with all that gang knowing about it, without having a pretty good idea of what might happen. He even says you expected it to happen, but of course that's stretching it. I can't see you conniving at murder."

"Give Mr. Stebbins my regards," Wolfe said, "and my thanks for the compliment."

"I will. Is that all you have to say?"

Wolfe slapped a palm on the desk. "What the devil do you expect me to say? Did you come here for the pleasure of screwing from me an admission that I bungled? I'll oblige you. I bungled. Anything else?"

"You're not a bungler." Cramer waved it away with the cigar. "Okay, we'll skip that; we might as well. What's bothering me is that the theory of the case the way we're going at it is based on something you know about and we don't. I've read Goodwin's statement three times. According to him, you decided that the three stories were all written by the same person, and it wasn't Alice Porter or Simon Jacobs or Jane Ogilvy. Is that correct?"

"It is."

"And you decided that by comparing them with books two of them had written and a transcript of Jane Ogilvy's testimony in court."

"Yes."

"Then we'd like to check it. I agree with Sergeant Stebbins that you're smart, I ought to know, but the whole approach depends on that, and naturally we want to check it. I understand that you have all that stuff here—the stories and the transcript and the books—and we want them. I'm no expert on writing myself, but we know a man who is. If this theory is right they'll probably be needed as evidence sooner or later. You have them?"

Wolfe nodded. "And I intend to keep them."

Cramer stuck the cigar between his lips and clamped his teeth on it. I had seen him light one only once, years ago. The cigar had a specific function, the idea being that with his teeth closed on it he couldn't speak the words that were on his tongue, and that gave him time to swallow them and substitute others. In five seconds he removed the cigar and said, "That's not reasonable."

"Mr. Cramer," Wolfe said. "Let's avoid a squabble if possible. The books are mine; you can get other copies elsewhere. The transcript and manuscripts belong to others and are in my care. I will surrender them only upon request from the owners. You can get them by court order only by establishing that they are material evidence, and I doubt if you can do that as things now stand. You can try."

"You goddam arrog—" Cramer stuck the cigar in his mouth and set his teeth on it. In four seconds he took it out. "Listen, Wolfe. Just answer a question. Would I be a sap if I worked a homicide case on a theory that rested entirely on something you and Goodwin said, not under oath?"

A corner of Wolfe's mouth twitched. That was his smile. "Yes," he said, "I must concede that. Perhaps we can resolve the difficulty. I offer a trade. In twenty-four hours you have doubtless gathered information that I would like to have. Give it to me. Then I will lend you what you came for, provided you sign an agreement to return it to me within twenty-four hours, intact."

"It would take all night to tell you all we've gathered."

"I don't want it all. Half an hour should do it, maybe less."

Cramer eyed him. "Forty-eight hours."

Wolfe's shoulders went up an eighth of an inch and down again. "I won't haggle. Very well, forty-eight. First and most important, have you discovered anything that contravenes the theory?"

"No."

"Have you discovered anything that suggests some other theory?"

"No."

"Have you discovered anything that supports the theory?"

"Only that the members of that committee verify Goodwin's statement. That doesn't prove you were right in the conclusion you made from reading that stuff, and that's why I want it. The widow knows nothing about it. She says. She also says that Jacobs had no enemies, that there couldn't have been anybody who had a reason to kill him except maybe one person, and that was a man named Goodwin who came to see him last Thursday. Because Jacobs told her to shut the door on him if he came again. We haven't asked Goodwin where he was Monday night from nine to eleven."

"I'm sure he appreciates your forbearance. Mr. Stebbins told Mr. Goodwin the period was nine to twelve."

"That was tentative. The stomach contents squeezed it a little. Nine to eleven."

"Good. Mr. Goodwin was here with me. Of course you have learned, or tried to, how many people knew of the plan to allure Jacobs. How many?"

"So far, forty-seven."

"They have all been spoken with?"

"All but two who are out of town."

"Do any of them merit attention?"

"They all do as long as we're on this theory. None of them especially. We haven't spotted anything that looks like a lead."

Wolfe grunted. "No wonder you want to confirm my conclusion. What about the routine? Is it still assumed that the body was taken there in a motor car?"

"Yes. Or a helicopter or a wheelbarrow."

Wolfe grunted again. "I am aware, Mr. Cramer, that you are too canny to jump to conclusions. I'll lump a hundred questions into one. Have you learned anything helpful from inspection of the scene, or examination of the body and clothing, or random inquiries?"

"Yes. That the blade of the knife was an inch wide and at least five inches long, that there was probably no struggle, and that he died between nine and eleven Monday night."

"Nothing else?"

"Nothing worth mentioning. Nothing to chew on."

"You have of course inquired about the payments made to Alice Porter, Simon Jacobs, and Jane Ogilvy, in settlement of the claims. If our theory is sound, substantial portions of those payments eventually found their way to another person."

"Certainly."

"Then who?"

"There is no record. In each case the check settling the claim was deposited and then a large amount was withdrawn in cash. We're still on that, but it looks hopeless."

"A moment ago, speaking of Mrs. Jacobs, you said, 'She says.' Do you question her candor?"

"No. I think she's straight."

"And she has no idea where her husband was going, or whom he was going to see, when he went out Monday evening?"

"No."

"Did he have anything with him that was not found on his body?"

"If he did she doesn't know it."

Wolfe shut his eyes. In a moment he opened them. "It is remarkable," he remarked, "how little a large group of competent trained investigators can gather in a night and a day. I intend no offense. You can't pick plums in a desert. Archie. Type this with two carbons: 'I acknowledge receipt of (list the items) from Nero Wolfe, as a personal loan to me. I guarantee to return all of the above-named items, intact, to Nero Wolfe not later than seven p.m. Friday, May 29th, 1959.' Make a package of the items."

"One thing," Cramer said. He put the cigar in the ashtray on the stand at his elbow. "You've got a client. That committee."

"Yes, sir."

"Okay, that's your business. My business is to investigate homicides as an officer of the law. I've answered your questions because you've got something I need and we made a deal, but that doesn't mean I'm sanctioning your horning in on *my* business. I've told you this before and I'm telling you again. Watch your step. Some day you're going to lose a leg, and don't expect me to give a damn."

"I won't." Wolfe eyed him. "I promise you, Mr. Cramer, that I will never plead your sanction to justify my conduct. My engagement with my client is to catch a swindler. Apparently he is also a murderer, and if so your claim will be superior. If and when I get him I'll bear that in mind. I don't suppose you challenge my right to expose a swindler?"

The rest of it was rather personal. I was busy typing the receipt and guarantee and then collecting the items and making the package, so I missed some of it. When I was tying the string it occurred to Cramer that he wanted to check the items against the list in the receipt, so I had to unwrap it, and then it occurred to him to ask about fingerprints on the manuscripts. You mustn't judge his abilities as a police inspector by that performance; Wolfe always has that effect on him. He gets behind.

When I returned to the office after letting him out it was only half an hour till dinnertime, and Wolfe had opened a book, not by a member of the committee, and was scowling at it, so I went for a walk. His brain works better when he is sitting down and mine when I am on my feet. Not that I would dream of comparing mine with his, though I do believe that in one or two respects—Oh, well.

Back in the office after dinner, and after coffee, I said politely that if I wasn't needed I would go and do a couple of personal errands. He asked if they were urgent, and I said no but I might as well get them done if we had nothing on hand.

"That's uncalled for," he growled. "Have you a suggestion?"

"No. None that I like."

"Neither have I. We have never been in a comparable situation. We can't explore motives; we know the motive. We can't set a trap; where would we put it? We can't ask questions of people; whom would we ask, and what? The forty-seven that Mr. Cramer's men have already seen and will see again? Pfui. Five hours for each would take ten hours a day for three weeks and more. We're almost as badly off as on Monday, when I told that confounded committee that it was no longer my kind of job and then idiotically consented to proceed with the plan proposed by Mr. Oshin. I admit it might have worked if we had taken proper precautions. Now Simon Jacobs is dead. I invite suggestions."

"Yeah. When I went for a walk you knew I wanted to think. I did. When I got back you knew from the expression on my face that I was empty, and I knew you were. The best I can do is remind you that thinking is your department. I haven't pestered you, have I? I know darned well it's a beaut."

"Then *I* have a suggestion. I don't like it, but we must either act or capitulate. You told Mr. Oshin on Monday that Jane Ogilvy might grab at the bait or she might spurn it. We have his ten thousand dollars and Mr. Dexter's offer to make any necessary contribution. It may be worth trying."

"It may," I conceded. "Wait till you see her."

"I'm not going to see her. That's for you. You are adept at dealing with personable young women, and I am not. Of course you will be severely handicapped. For Simon Jacobs you were provided with agreements by Richard Echols and Title House not to prosecute or demand reimbursement. You can't offer that inducement to Jane Ogilvy. She won her case in court, and even if we could get a similar agreement from Marjorie Lippin's heirs and from Nahm and Son, her publishers, which is doubtful, again our plan would be known to a number of people."

"Then it's a hell of a suggestion."

He nodded. "But it leads to another. From Jane Ogilvy's testimony at the trial, and from your report of your encounter with her, I gather that she is daft, and therefore unpredictable. Another approach might get her. Appeal to her sensibilities. Disclose the situation to her, all of it. Explain why we know that her claim against Marjorie Lippin was instigated by some person unknown to us, X. That X, threatened by imminent exposure, killed Simon Jacobs. Describe the grief and the plight of the widow and children; you might take her to see them and talk with them. Can you get a photograph of the corpse?"

"Probably, from Lon Cohen."

"Show it to her. Get one that shows the face, if possible; the face of a dead man before it has been rearranged is much more affecting than a mere heap of clothing. If you can't stir her sympathy perhaps you can arouse her fear. She is herself in peril; X may decide that she too must be removed. It would probably be a mistake to try to get her to supply evidence and details of her association with X, of the swindling of Marjorie Lippin; that would scare her off; all you really need is his name. Once we know him he is doomed. I want your opinion."

I glanced at the clock: ten minutes past nine. "It may take a while to find Lon. After seven o'clock there's no telling where he is. And the photograph would help."

"You think it's worth trying?"

"Sure. It may work. We've got to try something."

"We have indeed. Then as early in the morning as may be."

I turned to the phone and started after Lon Cohen.

Chapter 11

At a quarter to ten Thursday morning I braked the Heron sedan to a stop in front of 78 Haddon Place, Riverdale. Perhaps that wasn't "as early as may be," but I didn't want to tackle her before she had had breakfast, and besides, I hadn't been able to get the photograph until Lon got to the *Gazette* office at nine o'clock. As I was soon to learn, it didn't matter anyway, since she had already been dead about twelve hours.

If it had been a nice sunny morning I might have gone around to the side for a look at the terrace where I had found her before, but it was cloudy and cool, so I went up the walk to the entrance and pushed the button. The door was opened by a DAR type, a tall, upright female with a strong chin, in a gray dress with black buttons. Unquestionably the mother under whose devotion Jane had once been suffocating and probably still was.

"Good morning," she said.

"Good morning," I said. "My name is Archie Goodwin. Are you Mrs. Ogilvy?"

"I am."

"I would like to see your daughter, Miss Jane Ogilvy."

"Does she know you?"

"We have met. She may not recognize the name."

"She is in the cloister."

Good Lord, I thought, she has taken the veil. "Cloister?" I said.

"Yes. She may not be up yet. Go around the house to the left and from the terrace take the path through the shrubbery." She backstepped and was closing the door.

I followed directions. I had a feeling that I might have known she had a cloister—a cloister felt though not perceived. Rounding the house to the terrace, which was deserted, I took a graveled path which disappeared into bushes that gave it a roof. After winding among the bushes for some distance it left them and straightened out to pass between two big maples to the door of a small building—one story, gray stone, sloping roof, a curtained window on each side of the door. I proceeded and used the knocker, a big bronze flower with a red agate in the center. When nothing happened I knocked again, waited twenty seconds, turned the knob, found the door wasn't locked, opened it a couple of inches, and called through the crack, "Miss Ogilvy!" No response. I swung the door open and stepped in.

It was a fine well-furnished cloister and probably contained many objects that were worth a look, but my attention centered immediately on its tenant. She was on her back on the floor in front of an oversized couch, dressed in a blue garment that I would call a smock but she probably had called something else. One of her legs was bent a little, but the other one was out straight. Crossing to her, I stooped to get her hand

and found that the arm was completely stiff. I got a foot, which was covered by a sock but no shoe; the leg was stiff too. She had been dead a minimum of six hours, and almost certainly more.

There was a dark red stain at heart level around a slit in the smock, not a big one. My hand started to open the zipper for a look underneath. But I drew it back. Let the medical examiner do it. I straightened up and looked around. There was no sign of a struggle or of any disturbance—no drawers open or anything scattered around. Everything was as it should be except that she was dead.

I said aloud, with feeling, "The sonofabitch."

There was a phone on a table against a wall, and I went and lifted the receiver, using my handkerchief, and put it to my ear. The dial tone came. There was a chance that it was an extension, but probably not; the number on the disk was not the same as the one listed for Ogilvy in the phone book. I dialed and got Fritz, and asked him to buzz the plant rooms.

Wolfe's voice: "Yes?"

I apologized. "I'm sorry to disturb you so often when you're up with the orchids, but I've hit another snag. I'm in a building in the rear of the Ogilvy grounds which Jane called the cloister. Her corpse is here on the floor. Stabbed in the chest. She died at least six hours ago, probably more. At the house her mother told me she was here and might not be up yet, and I came here alone. I have touched nothing but the knocker and the doorknob. If you want me to hurry home for new instructions, okay, I knocked a few times and got no response, and left. I can stop at the house and tell Mrs. Ogilvy that."

He growled, "If you had gone last night."

"Yeah. Maybe. She was probably killed about the

time I started trying to find Lon Cohen. If I leave I should leave quick."

"Why leave? How in the name of heaven could I have new instructions?"

"I thought you might want to discuss the situation."

"Pfui. Discussion wouldn't help it any."

"Then I stick."

"Yes."

He hung up. I cradled the phone, considered for half a minute, stepped to the door and on out, shut the door, wiped the knob with my handkerchief, followed the path back to the house and around to the front entrance, and pushed the button. Again the door was opened by the devoted mother.

"I'm sorry to bother you again," I said, "but I thought I ought to tell you. Miss Ogilvy doesn't seem to be there. I knocked several times, and knocked loud, and got no response."

She wasn't alarmed. "She must be there. She hasn't been in for breakfast."

"I knocked hard."

"Then she's gone somewhere. There's a lane in back of the cloister, and she keeps her car there."

"Gone without breakfast?"

"She might. She never has, but she might."

I took a chance. It was highly unlikely that X had gone off with her car. "What make is her car?"

"Jaguar."

"It's there. I looked around a little and saw it. I think you ought to come and see, Mrs. Ogilvy. She might have had a stroke or something."

"She doesn't have strokes. I never go to the cloister." She tightened her lips. "But perhaps I should— All right. You come along."

She crossed the sill and shut the door, and I moved aside to let her by. She strode like a female sergeant, around to the terrace and across it, and along the path. When she reached the door of the cloister she started her hand for the knob, but changed her mind and raised it to the knocker. She knocked three times, at intervals, turned her head to look at me, grabbed the knob and opened the door, and entered. I followed. In three steps she saw it and stopped. I said something, went on by, on to it, squatted, and touched an arm. I unzipped the smock, spread it open, and took a look.

I stood up. Mother hadn't moved, except that her mouth was working. "She's dead," I said. "Stabbed in the chest. She has been dead quite a while."

"So she did it," Mrs. Ogilvy said.

"No. Someone else did it. There's no weapon."

"It's under her. It's somewhere."

"No. If she did it and pulled the weapon out, still alive, there would be a lot of blood, and there is almost none. It was pulled out after her heart stopped."

"You know a lot about it."

"I know that much. Will you call the police or shall I?"

"She did it."

"No. She did not."

"Who are you?"

"My name is Archie Goodwin. I'm a private detective. I've had some experience with death by violence."

"Do you mean she was murdered?"

"Yes."

"Are you sure?"

"Yes."

"Thank God." She turned her head, saw a chair,

went to it, and sat. She started to slump, then jerked her shoulders back. "Then you must call the police?"

"Certainly." I had moved to face her. "It might help if I could give them some information on the phone. Could you answer a few questions?"

"If I choose to."

"When did you last see your daughter?"

"When she left the house last evening to come here."

"What time was that?"

"Right after dinner. Half past eight—a little later."

"Was anyone with her?"

"No."

"Did she always sleep here?"

"Not always. Frequently. She has her room in the house."

"Were there guests at dinner?"

"No. Just my husband and I, and her."

"Was she expecting someone to call?"

"Not that I knew of, but I wouldn't. I seldom did."

"You know nothing of any letter or phone call she got yesterday?"

"No. I wouldn't."

"Did anyone come to see her after she left the house last evening, or call her on the phone?"

"No. Not at the house. Someone might have come here."

"Someone did. How? By the lane in back?"

"Yes. It's a public road. Dipper Lane. I've forgotten your name. What is it?"

"Goodwin. Archie Goodwin. Did you hear a car on the lane last evening, stopping here or starting here?"

"No." Abruptly she left the chair. "I'm going to phone my husband. He should be here when the police come. How soon will they come?"

"Ten minutes, maybe less. Have you any idea who killed your daughter? Any idea at all?"

"No." She turned and marched out, still a sergeant.

I went to the phone, used my handkerchief to lift the receiver, and dialed.

Chapter 12

I ate lunch that day, two hamburgers and a glass of milk, at the office of the Bronx District Attorney, in the room of an assistant DA named Halloran whom I had never seen before. I ate dinner, if two corned-beef sandwiches and lukewarm coffee in a paper cup can be called dinner, in the office of the District Attorney of the County of New York, in the room of an assistant DA named Mandelbaum whom I knew quite well from various contacts on other occasions. When I finally got back to the old brownstone on West 35th Street it was going on ten o'clock. Fritz offered to warm up the lamb loaf and said it would be edible, but I told him I was too tired to eat and might nibble a snack later.

It was nearly eleven when I finished reporting to Wolfe. Actually I knew very little more than I had when Mrs. Ogilvy had left the cloister and I had dialed SP 7-3100, but Wolfe was now trying to find a straw to grab at. He wanted everything I had, every sight and sound of my twelve-hour day, even including the session at the Bronx DA's office, though Halloran had known nothing of the background. He had me repeat my conversation with Mrs. Ogilvy three times. He almost never asks me to repeat anything even once, but of course he was desperate. When there was nothing left to ask me he still had a question; he wanted to know what conclusions I had drawn.

I shook my head. "You draw the conclusions. I only make guesses. I guess we might as well quit. I guess this bird is too fast and too slick. I guess he hasn't left one little crumb for the cops, either with Simon Jacobs or Jane Ogilvy, and as for us, I guess he's a step ahead and intends to stay ahead. I guess we had better consider how to approach Alice Porter so we can get to her a little sooner than we have the others—say when she's been dead only an hour or two."

Wolfe grunted. "I have already considered her."

"Good. Then she may still be warm."

"I have also acted. Saul and Fred and Orrie have her under surveillance. Also Miss Bonner and that operative in Miss Bonner's employ. Miss Corbett."

My brows went up. "You don't say. Since when?"

"Shortly after you called this morning. Orrie is there now. Since four o'clock he has been there in concealment with the house in view. His car is nearby, also in concealment. Miss Corbett, with a rented car, is posted near the junction of the dirt road and the surfaced road. Saul will relieve Orrie at midnight, and Miss Corbett will leave. Fred and Miss Bonner will take over at eight in the morning. Miss Corbett phoned at seven-thirty that Alice Porter was at home and had had no visitors."

My brows were still up. "I must say that when you consider, you consider. At that rate Oshin's ten grand won't last long. I don't say it's being wasted, but you may remember that when he asked me which one of the four we should go for I said that Alice Porter has just made her claim on Amy Wynn and is expecting to collect, so she probably wouldn't be open for a deal. Also you know how she reacted to my approach."

Wolfe nodded. "But that was before her manuscript had been found and we learned that it had been written by her, not by the person who wrote the others. He may or may not know about that; probably he does. In any case, even if it is likely that she would scorn any inducement we can offer her, he may not think so. He is bold and ruthless, and he is now close to panic. If he thinks her as great a menace as Jane Ogilvy he won't hesitate. Saul and Fred and Orrie, and Miss Bonner and Miss Corbett, have full instructions. Anyone who approaches Alice Porter is to be suspected. If possible he is to be stopped before he strikes, but of course he can't be challenged until it is apparent that he intends to strike."

"Yeah." I was looking at it. "It's a problem. Fred or Orrie is there, in broad daylight, and someone drives up to the house and goes in. There's no decent cover within a hundred yards of the house. He can't possibly get close enough to see if it's just a lightning-rod salesman or a friend, without being seen. All he can do is wait until the company goes and then wait for Alice Porter to show, or go to a phone and dial her number and see if she answers. If it's X, she's a goner. I admit we'll have him."

He grunted. "Can you do better?"

"No, sir. I'm not complaining. What about Kenneth Rennert? If X is in a panic he might do him next."

"That's possible, but I doubt it. Rennert may not even know who X is; he may merely have imitated him. He wrote not a story but a play outline, and we haven't seen it."

"Okay." I glanced at the clock: 11:23. "I suppose

Saul will call when he goes on at midnight, and Orrie will call after he is relieved?"

"Yes."

"I'll expect them. What else for me? Have I a program?"

"No."

"Then I have a suggestion. I don't like it, but I have it. Across the street from Rennert's address is a tailor shop with a nice clean window. For five bucks a day the owner would let me use it to look through, with a chair to sit on. After dark I could move across the street, to be closer. I am almost as good as Paul Panzer at remembering faces. When Rennert's body is discovered and they decide when he was killed, I would know who had been there. If it was someone I recognized, for instance a member of the Joint Committee on Plagiarism, I could even name him. I can start right now. I hate that kind of a job, who doesn't, but I've been sent twice now to see people who were already dead, and that's enough."

He shook his head. "Two objections. One, you need sleep. Two, Mr. Rennert is not at home. As I said, his operation may have been solely on his own and he may have had no connection with X, but I haven't ignored him. I rang his number twice this morning and twice this afternoon, and got no answer. At three o'clock Saul went there, and, getting no response to his ring, saw the building superintendent and asked when he had last seen Mr. Rennert. Early last evening Mr. Rennert told the building superintendent that he would leave today to spend the Memorial Day weekend in the country and would return on Monday. He didn't say where in the country."

"If we knew where we could ring him and warn

him to keep away from poison ivy. It would be nice to hear his voice."

"I agree. But we don't."

"I could scout around in the morning and probably find out. We have a lot of names of people he has borrowed money from."

He vetoed it. He said he wanted me at hand, and a call might come at any time of the day or night from Saul Panzer or Fred Durkin or Orrie Cather or Dol Bonner or Sally Corbett that would require immediate action. Also Philip Harvey had phoned twice, and Cora Ballard once, to ask if he could be present at a meeting of the NAAD council on Monday, and they would probably phone again tomorrow, and he didn't want to listen to them. That settled, he went up to bed. At 11:42 Saul Panzer called, from a booth in Carmel, to say that he was on his way to relieve Orrie Cather. At 12:18 Orrie called, also from Carmel, to report that the light had gone out a little before eleven in Alice Porter's house, and presumably she was safe in bed. I mounted two flights to mine.

Friday morning I was pulling my pants on when Fred Durkin phoned that he was on his way to relieve Saul, and Dol Bonner was with him, to go on post near the junction of the blacktop and the dirt road. I was in the kitchen, pouring hot maple syrup on a waffle, with the *Times* propped on the rack, when Saul phoned to say that when he left at eight o'clock Alice Porter had been hoeing in the vegetable garden. I was in the office, rereading copies of the statements I had given the two assistant DAs, when Cora Ballard phoned to ask if Wolfe would come to the NAAD council meeting, which would be held at the Clover Club on Monday at twelve-thirty. If Wolfe preferred to join them after lunch two o'clock would do, or even two-thirty. When I reminded her that he never left the house on business she said she knew that, but this was an emergency. I said it wasn't much of an emergency that set a meeting three days off, and she said that with authors and dramatists two or three weeks was the best she could usually do, and anyway it was the Memorial Day weekend, and could she speak with Mr. Wolfe. I told her he wasn't available and it wouldn't do any good even if he was, and what he would certainly say was that he would send me. If they wanted me, let me know.

I was filing the copies of the statements in the folder marked PLAGIARISM, JOINT COMMITTEE ON when Inspector Cramer phoned to say that he would drop in for a few minutes about a quarter past eleven. I told him he would probably be admitted. I was listening to the ten-o'clock news broadcast when Lon Cohen phoned to say it was high time I loosened up. They had five different pictures of me in the morgue, and they would run the best one, the one that made me look almost human, as the discoverer of Jane Ogilvy's body, if I would supply some interesting detail like why had two people who had collected damages on plagiarism charges been croaked within forty-eight hours. Any fool knew damn well it wasn't coincidence, so what was it? I told him I would ask the DA and call him back.

I was tearing yesterday's page from Wolfe's desk calendar when the president of the National Association of Authors and Dramatists phoned. His name was Jerome Tabb. I had read one of his books. Wolfe had read four of them, and all four were still on the shelves, none of them dog-eared. They had all been A's. He was a VIP even by Wolfe's standards, and Wolfe would undoubtedly have liked to speak with him, but the rule was never buzz the plant rooms for a phone call except in extreme emergency. Tabb had just had a call from Cora Ballard, and he wanted to tell Wolfe how important it was for him to be present at the council meeting on Monday. He was leaving town for the weekend, and he would like me to give Wolfe this message, that the officers and council of the NAAD would deeply appreciate it if he would arrange to meet with them.

When Wolfe came down at eleven I reported the phone calls in chronological order, which put Tabb last. When I finished he sat and glared at me but said nothing. He was stuck. He knew that I knew he would like to speak with Jerome Tabb, but he couldn't very well jump me for obeying the rules. So he took another tack. Glaring at me, he said, "You were too emphatic with Miss Ballard and Mr. Tabb. I may decide to go to that meeting." Absolutely childish. It called for a cutting reply, and one was on its way to my tongue when the doorbell rang and I had to skip it.

It was Cramer. When I opened the door he marched by me with no greeting but an excuse for a nod, and on to the office. I followed. Wolfe told him good morning and invited him to sit, but he stood.

"I've only got a minute," he said. "So your theory was right."

Wolfe grunted. "My theory and yours."

"Yeah. It's too bad that Ogilvy girl had to die to prove it."

He stopped. Wolfe asked, "Will you sit? As you know, I like eyes at a level."

"I can't stay. The Ogilvy homicide was in the Bronx, but obviously it's tied in with Jacobs', so it's mine. You can save me a lot of time and trouble. If we have to we can find out from about fifty people how many of them you told that you were going to put the squeeze on Jane Ogilvy, and which ones, but it's simpler to ask you. So I'm asking."

"Mr. Goodwin has already answered that question several times. To the District Attorney."

"I know he has, and I don't believe him. I think you bungled again. I think you picked certain people out of the bunch that had known you were going after Jacobs —I don't know how you picked them, but you do—you picked certain ones and let them know you were going after Jane Ogilvy. Then you sent a man or men, probably Panzer and Durkin, to cover her, and they slipped up. Maybe they didn't know about that lane in back. Maybe they didn't even know about that building she called the cloister. Cloister my ass. I want to know who you told and why. If you won't tell me I'll find out the hard way, and when we get this cleared up and we know which one killed her, and we know he killed her because he knew you were going after her, and he knew because you or Goodwin had told him, this will be the time you lose a leg. I've got just one question: are you going to tell me?"

"I'll answer it in a moment." Wolfe wiggled a finger at him. "First I remind you that you are to return that stuff to me by seven o'clock this evening—less than eight hours from now. You haven't forgotten that?"

"No. You'll have it."

"Good. As for your question, I don't resent it. I blundered so lamentably with Simon Jacobs that it's no wonder you suspect me of an even bigger blunder with Jane Ogilvy. If I had I would confess it, abandon the case, and close my office permanently. I didn't. No one knew of our intention to tackle Jane Ogilvy but Mr. Goodwin and me."

"So you're not telling."

"There's nothing to tell. Mr. Goodwin has—"

"Go to hell." He turned and marched out. I went to the hall to see that when the door banged he was outside. As I stepped back in the phone rang. It was Mortimer Oshin, wanting to know if Philip Harvey had notified Wolfe that his arrangement with the committee was terminated. I said no, apparently that was to be discussed by the NAAD council on Monday. He said that if and when it was terminated he wanted to engage Wolfe personally, and I said it was nice to know that.

Wolfe, not bothering to comment on Cramer, told me to take my notebook and dictated a letter to a guy in Chicago, declining a request to come and give a talk at the annual banquet of the Midwest Association of Private Inquiry Agents. Then one, a long one, to a woman in Nebraska who had written to ask if it was possible to fatten a capon so that its liver would make as good a pâté as that of a fattened goose. Then others. I agree in principle with his notion that no letter should go unanswered, but of course he can always hand one to me and say, "Answer that," and often does. We were on one to a man in Atlanta, saying that he couldn't undertake to find a daughter who had left for New York a month ago and had never written, when Fritz announced lunch. As we were crossing the hall the phone rang, and I went back to get it. It was Fred Durkin.

"I'm in Carmel." He had his mouth too close to the transmitter, as usual. He's a good operative, but he has his faults. "The subject left the house at twelve forty-two and got in her car and drove off. She had been wearing slacks, but she had changed to a dress. I had to wait till she was out of sight to leave cover, then I went to my car and followed, but of course she was gone. Dol Bonner's car wasn't at her post, so she picked her up. Neither of their cars is parked here in the center of town. Shall I ask around to find out which way they went?"

"No. Go back and hide your car again and take cover. Somebody might come and wait there for her."

"It's a hell of a long wait."

"Yeah, I know. The first two weeks are the hardest. Study nature. There's plenty of it around there."

I joined Wolfe in the dining room, took my seat, and relayed the news. He grunted and picked up his napkin.

An hour and ten minutes later we were back in the office, finishing with the mail, when the phone interrupted; and when a soft but businesslike voice said, "This is Dol Bonner," I motioned to Wolfe to get on.

"Yes, Miss Bonner," I said. "Where are you?"

"In a phone booth in a drugstore. At twelve forty-nine the subject's car came out of the dirt road and turned left on the blacktop. I followed. She went to the Taconic State Parkway, no stops, and headed south. At Hawthorne Circle she took the Saw Mill River. I nearly lost her twice but got her again. She left the West Side Highway at Nineteenth Street. She put her car in a parking lot on Christopher Street and walked here, five blocks. I found a space at the curb."

"Where is here?"

"This drugstore is at the corner of Arbor Street and Bailey Street. She went in the vestibule at Forty-two Arbor Street and pushed a button, and waited half a minute, and opened the door and entered. That was eight minutes ago. I can't see the entrance from the booth, so if you want—"

"Did you say Forty-two?"

"Yes."

"Hold it." I turned to Wolfe. "Amy Wynn lives at Forty-two Arbor Street."

"Indeed. This is Nero Wolfe, Miss Bonner. Can you see the entrance from where your car is parked?"

"Yes."

"Then go to your car. If she comes out, follow her. Mr. Goodwin will join you if you're still there when he arrives. Satisfactory?"

We hung up. We looked at each other. "Nonsense," Wolfe growled.

"Close to it," I agreed. "But it's possible. You told them Wednesday that it could be that one of them was it. If I had voted, Amy Wynn wouldn't have been my choice, but it's possible. Simon Jacobs was no athlete. If she had him in a car she could have sunk a knife in him. Certainly Jane Ogilvy would have been no problem. And for Alice Porter she has a double motive—not only to keep her from blabbing the Ellen Sturdevant operation but also to settle the claim Alice Porter has made against *her*. That's one way to settle a claim out of court. I wouldn't think she would pick her own apartment as the best place for it, but you said she was close to panic—only you said 'he.' Also she might have some original and nifty plan for getting rid of a body. She or he is quite a planner, you can't deny that. I could go and drop in on her and say I'm making the rounds of the committee members, to ask them not to fire you. If I was too late to save Alice Porter's life I would at least be in time to interfere with her body-disposal plan."

"Pfui."

"Cramer won't think it's phooey if Alice Porter is number three, another homicide in his jurisdiction, and he learns that you had Dol Bonner there in a car with her eye on the door. Your crack about closing your office permanently may turn out—"

The phone rang, and I got it. It was Reuben Imhof. He asked for Wolfe, and Wolfe got on.

"Something interesting," Imhof said. "I just had a phone call from Amy Wynn. Alice Porter rang her this morning and said she wanted to come and see her. If Miss Wynn had told me about it, I would probably have advised her not to see her, but she didn't. Anyway, Alice Porter is there with her now, in her apartment. She offers to settle her claim for twenty thousand dollars cash. Miss Wynn wants to know if I think she should accept the offer. I told her no. It looks to me as if the two murders have got Alice Porter scared. She suspects they were committed by the man who got her to make the claim on Ellen Sturdevant, and if he's caught he may talk, and she'll be sunk, and she wants to get what she can quick and clear out. What do you think?"

"You are probably correct. My offhand opinion."

"Yes. That's the way it looks. But after I hung up I wasn't so sure I had given Miss Wynn good advice. Alice Porter would probably take half the amount she named, even less. If Miss Wynn can get a general release for, say, five thousand dollars perhaps that's what she ought to do. If she doesn't she may eventually have to pay ten times that, or more. On the other hand, if you or the police get the man you're after and rip it open, she won't have to pay anything. So I'm asking you. Shall I call Miss Wynn and advise her to make a deal if she can get one for ten thousand or less, or not?"

Wolfe grunted. "You can't expect me to answer that. Miss Wynn is not my client, and neither are you.

As a member of the committee you may ask me if I expect to expose that swindler and murderer."

"All right, I do."

"The answer is yes. Soon or late, he is doomed."

"That suits me. Then I won't call her."

Wolfe cradled the phone and gave me a look, with a corner of his mouth slanting up.

"Okay." I left my chair. "I only said it was possible. Would it be a good idea for me to help Dol Bonner tail her back to Carmel?"

"No."

"Any special instructions for Miss Bonner?"

"No. Presumably she will find Miss Corbett at her post."

I bet it.

Chapter 13

Forty-two hours later, at nine o'clock Sunday morning, as I put down my empty coffee cup, thanked Fritz for the meal, and headed for the office, I told myself aloud, "What a hell of a way to spend a Memorial Day weekend." I had been invited to the country. I had been invited to a boat in the Sound. I had been invited to accompany a friend to Yankee Stadium that afternoon. And here I was. The only reason I was up and dressed was that the phone had roused me at twenty to eight, Fred calling to say that he was on his way to relieve Saul; and half an hour later Saul had reported that Alice Porter slept late on Sunday, which was the most exciting piece of news I had heard for quite a while. On Friday, tailed by Dol Bonner, she had driven from Arbor Street straight back to Carmel, done some shopping at a supermarket and a drugstore, and then home.

Entering the office, I went to my desk and started to plow through the mountain of the Sunday *Times*—my copy; Wolfe's was up in his room—for the section I looked at first. I yanked it out, scowled at it, said aloud, "Oh nuts," and tossed it on the floor. Either I had meant it when I thought to myself last night, as I sat watching a cowboy take off his boots and wiggle his toes on TV, that it would be more interesting to be in jail, or I hadn't. If I had it was up to me. I would be losing nothing if I got nabbed for a misdemeanor or even a minor felony. I went to the phone, dialed the number of Kenneth Rennert's apartment, got no answer after thirteen rings, and hung up. I went to a cabinet and unlocked a drawer, took out six boxes of assorted keys, and spent twenty minutes making selections. From another drawer I got a pair of rubber gloves. I went to the kitchen and told Fritz I was going for a walk and would be back in an hour or so, and left the house. It was only a twenty-minute stroll.

I was not actually determined to get tossed in the coop. I thought I might find something helpful in Rennert's nice big room. I knew from past experience that Wolfe would have approved, but if I had told him in advance he would have been responsible, me being his agent, and it was fair for him to share the risk of my law-breaking when it was his idea, but not when it was mine. I wasn't hoping to find evidence that Rennert was X, but there was a chance of digging up something to indicate that X had instigated his claim against Mortimer Oshin, or that he hadn't. Either one would help a little, and I might get more.

After pushing the Rennert button in the vestibule three times, with waits between, and getting no reaction, I started to work on the door. My position on locks is about the same as on fingerprints—I couldn't qualify as an expert witness, but I have picked up a lot of pointers. Of course I had noticed on my previous visit that the street-door lock and the one upstairs were both Hansens. Anywhere and everywhere you go you should always notice the kind of lock, in case it becomes necessary at some future time to get in without help.

Hansens are good locks, but I had a good assortment. I was under no pressure; if someone had appeared from either direction, I was merely using the wrong key. In three minutes, maybe less, I got it and was inside. The elevator wasn't there; I pushed the button to bring it down, entered, and pushed the "4" button. The door to the apartment took longer than the one downstairs because I was too stubborn in trying to make the same key do, but finally I had it. I swung the door gently six inches and stood with my ear cocked. At that hour Sunday morning Rennert might have ignored the phone and the doorbell. Hearing nothing except traffic sounds from the street, I swung the door farther and entered the nice big room.

He was lying on the nice big couch, on his back. One swift glance, even from a distance, was enough to show that he wasn't asleep. His face was so swollen that no one would have dreamed of calling him handsome, and the handle of a knife was protruding from his chest, which was bare because the dressing gown he had on was open in front down to the belt. I crossed over. The skin of his belly was green. I pressed a finger on the skin at a couple of spots below the ribs; it was tight and rubbery. I put on the rubber gloves and removed one of his slippers and tried the toes; they were flabby. I bent over to get my nose an inch from his open mouth and inhaled; once was enough. He had been dead at least two days, and probably three or four.

I looked around; no sign of a disturbance or search. On a stand near the head of the couch were a half-full bottle of bourbon, two tall glasses, a pack of cigarettes, a book of matches with the flap open, and an ashtray with nothing in it. Having made a guess, that a guy of Rennert's build and condition wouldn't lie quietly on his back while someone stuck a knife in him unless he had been somehow processed, which was sound, I stopped to smell the glasses, which was dumb. The best-known drug for a Mickey Finn has almost no taste or odor, and even if it had, it couldn't be detected by the naked nose after three or four days.

The knife handle was brown plastic. I made another guess, as to why the weapon had been left in place this time, and to check it I crossed to an arch through which a refrigerator could be seen, and looked in. It was a nice little kitchenette. The second drawer I opened contained, among other items, two knives with brown plastic handles, one with a three-inch blade and one with a five-inch. The blade in Rennert's chest was probably seven-inch. That supported my other guess. You don't sneak a knife from your host's kitchen drawer and take it to the living room to kill him with if his eyes are open and his muscles usable.

Having made two good guesses, I decided that would do for a Sunday morning. The idea of spending a couple of hours going over the place, even with rubber gloves, didn't appeal to me. Being found in a man's castle which you have entered illegally can be embarrassing, but if he is there with you with a knife in his chest, even if he has started to decompose, it can be really ticklish. I decided that I hadn't *really* meant it when I thought it would be more interesting to be in jail. Besides, I had told Fritz I would be back in an hour or so.

I left. I used my handkerchief to wipe the only things I had touched with my bare fingers: the knob of the apartment door, the elevator door, and the button in the elevator. Before starting the elevator down I took off the rubber gloves and stuffed them in my pocket. Everything under control. I would wipe the button on the panel downstairs.

But I didn't. When the elevator stopped at the bottom, naturally I took a look through the square of glass before I opened the door. No one was in view in the lobby, but in a tenth of a second there would be. The door to the vestibule was being pushed open from the outside by a little guy in his shirt sleeves, and towering behind him was the big square face of Sergeant Purley Stebbins. At a moment like that you don't use your head because there isn't time. You use your finger, to press the "2" button in the elevator. Which I did. Electricity is wonderful; the elevator started up. When it stopped at the second floor, I stepped out. When the door closed, the elevator started down, showing that someone had pushed the button in the lobby. Really wonderful.

I stood in the little hall. It was now a question of odds. There was one chance in a thousand trillion that Purley would get out at the second floor, but if he did all the gods in heaven obviously had it in for me and I was sunk no matter what I did. The elevator went on by, and I made for the stairs. There was one chance in a thousand that the shirt-sleeved guy, who had to be the janitor—I beg his pardon, building superintendent —had stayed in the lobby instead of going up with Purley to let him in Rennert's apartment, but if so only a couple of minor gods were against me, and I could cope with them. I descended and found the lobby empty. Now the odds were the other way. It was fifty to one that there was a police car outside with a man in it, and ten to one that if I emerged to the sidewalk he would see me. That was simple; I didn't emerge. I went to the vestibule and pressed the button by Rennert's name and took the receiver from the hook. In a moment a voice came. "Who is it?"

I told the grill, "It's Archie Goodwin, Mr. Rennert. You may remember I was here ten days ago. You didn't like the deal I offered, but I've got a new angle that makes it different. I think you ought to hear it. I'm pretty sure it will appeal to you."

"All right, come on up."

The buzz sounded, and I opened the door and entered, went to the elevator, and pushed the button to bring it down. That button wouldn't have to be wiped now. When it came I stepped in and pushed the "4" button. When I got out at the fourth floor my face was ready with a friendly grin for Rennert, but at sight of Sergeant Stebbins my mouth opened in shocked surprise and I gawked.

"Not *you*," I said.

"This is just too goddam pat," he said. He sounded a little hoarse. He whirled to Shirt-sleeves, who was in the doorway. "Take a look at this man. Have you seen him hanging around?"

"No, Sergeant, I haven't." The building superintendent looked a little sick. "I never saw him before. Excuse me, I've got to—"

"Don't touch anything in there!"

"Then I've got to—" He dashed to the stairs and was gone.

"I wish I *had* been hanging around," I said. "I might have seen the murderer enter or leave, or both. How long has Rennert been dead?"

"How do you know he's dead?"

"Now come. Not only you here and the mood you're in, but also him looking for somewhere to puke. Was it today? Was he stabbed like the others?"

He advanced a step, to arm's length. "I want to

know exactly why you came here at exactly this time."
He was hoarser. "I had been at that Jacobs place five
minutes, and there you came. I've been here three
minutes, and here you come. You didn't come to see
Rennert. You'd ring his number first to see if he was
here. You knew damn well it wasn't him that asked
you who it is. You knew it was me. You're good on
voices. And you're good at lies, and I've had enough of
'em. *You* puke. Puke a little truth."

"You would too," I said.

"I would too what?"

"Ring his number first. And when you ring a number and get no answer, do you always assume that the
ringee is dead and go to see? I should hope not. Why
did *you* come here at exactly this time?"

His jaw worked. "Okay, I'll tell you. The janitor got
a phone call Friday from the people where Rennert
was supposed to go for the weekend, and another one
yesterday. He thought Rennert had just decided to go
somewhere else, and he didn't want to enter the apartment, but he phoned the Missing Persons Bureau.
They thought it was just another false alarm, but this
morning someone at the bureau remembered he had
seen Rennert's name on a report and called us. Now
it's your turn, and by God, I want it straight! And
fast!"

I was frowning thoughtfully. "It's too bad," I said,
"that I always seem to rub you the wrong way. As
sore as you are, the best thing you could do would be
to take me down and book me, but I don't know what
for. It's not even a misdemeanor to ring a man's doorbell. What I would like to do is help, since I'm here. If
you've only been here three minutes you haven't had
time to try all the tests, and maybe he's not dead. I'd
be glad to—"

"Get going!" His hands were fists, and a muscle at the side of his neck was working. "Get!"

I didn't take the elevator. Purley knew that the natural thing would be for me to find the janitor and pump him, so I took the stairs. He had made it all the way to the basement. I found him there, pale and upset. He was too sick to talk, or too scared, or he may have thought I was the murderer. I told him the best thing was strong hot tea, no sugar, found my way to the sidewalk, and headed for home. I walked, taking my time. There was no point in disturbing Wolfe in the plant rooms, since there was no emergency. Rennert's belly had already turned green, and another half an hour wouldn't matter.

I had returned the keys and rubber gloves to the drawers, and fixed myself a gin and tonic because I wanted to swallow something and the idea of milk or water didn't seem to appeal to my stomach, and was looking at the sports section of the *Times* when Wolfe came down. We exchanged good mornings, and he went to the only chair in the world he really approved of, sat, rang for beer, and said I might as well go for a walk. He has some sort of an idea that my going for a walk is good for him.

"I already have," I told him. "I found another corpse, this time in an advanced condition. Kenneth Rennert."

"I'm in no mood for flummery. Take a walk."

"No flummery." I put the paper down. "I dialed Rennert's number and got no answer. I walked to his address and rang the bell and got no answer. Happening to have keys and rubber gloves with me, and thinking I might find something interesting, I went in and up to his apartment. For three or four days he has been lying on a couch with a knife in his chest, and is still there. So is the knife. He was probably fed a dose in a drink before—"

I stopped because he was having a fit. He had closed his right hand to make a fist and was hitting the desk with it, and he was bellowing. He was roaring something in a language that was probably the one he had used as a boy in Montenegro, the one that he and Marko Vukcic had sometimes talked. He had roared like that when he heard that Marko had been killed, and on three other occasions over the years. Fritz, entering with beer, stopped and looked at me reproachfully. Wolfe quit bellowing as abruptly as he had started, glared at Fritz, and said coldly, "Take that back. I don't want it."

"But it will do—"

"Take it back. I shall drink no beer until I get my fingers around the creature's throat. And I shall eat no meat."

"But impossible! The squabs are marinating!"

"Throw them out."

"Wait a minute," I objected. "What about Fritz and Theodore and me? Okay, Fritz. We've had a shock. I shall eat no boiled cucumbers."

Fritz opened his mouth, closed it again, turned, and went. Wolfe, his fists on the desk, commanded me, "Report."

Six minutes would have been enough for it, but I thought it would be well to give him time to calm down a little, so I stretched it to ten, and when I ran out of facts I continued, "I would want full price, no discount, for my two guesses—that the knife came from his kitchen drawer, and that he was drugged, unconscious, when he was stabbed. I have another guess on which I'd allow five per cent off for cash, no more—that he had been dead eighty hours. Between eighty and eighty-five. He was killed late Wednesday night. X went straight to him after killing Jane Ogilvy. If he had put it off until after the news about Jane Ogilvy was out, Rennert would have been too much on his guard to let X put something in his drink. Rennert may or may not have suspected that X had killed Simon Jacobs, since nothing had been published connecting his death with the plagiarism charge he had made three years ago. But if Rennert had known about Jane Ogilvy too, he certainly would have suspected. Hell, he would have known. So X couldn't wait, and he didn't. He went to Rennert to discuss their claim against Mortimer Oshin, knowing that Rennert would offer him a drink. He offered me one before I had been in his place three minutes."

I stopped for breath. Wolfe opened his fists and worked his fingers.

"Three comments," I said. "First, one question is answered—whether Rennert's operation was independent or was one of X's string. X has answered that for us. I admit it doesn't help any, with Rennert dead, but it makes it neater, and you like things neat. Second, with Rennert dead, his claim against Mortimer Oshin is dead too, and Oshin may want his ten grand back, and the committee may fire you tomorrow, and the Alice Porter surveillance is costing over three hundred bucks a day. Third, your beer and meat pledge. We'll ignore it. You were temporarily off your nut. This is tough enough as it is, and with you starving and dying of thirst it would be impossible." I left my chair. "I'll bring the beer."

"No." He made fists again. "I have committed myself. Sit down."

"God help us," I said, and sat.

Chapter 14

We were in conference, off and on, all the rest of the day, with time out for meals. The meals were dismal. Squab marinated in light cream, rolled in flour seasoned with salt, pepper, nutmeg, clove, thyme, and crushed juniper berries, sautéed in olive oil, and served on toast spread with red currant jelly, with Madeira cream sauce poured over it, is one of Wolfe's favorite tidbits. He ordinarily consumes three of them, though I have known him to make it four. That day I wanted to eat in the kitchen, but no. I had to sit and down my two while he grimly pecked away at his green peas and salad and cheese. The Sunday-evening snack was just as bad. He usually has something like cheese and anchovy spread or pâté de foie gras or herring in sour cream, but apparently the meat pledge included fish. He ate crackers and cheese and drank four cups of coffee. Later, in the office, he finished off a bowl of pecans, and then went to the kitchen for a brush and pan to collect the bits of shell on his desk and the rug. He sure was piling on the agony.

In the state he was in now, he would have been willing to try one or more of the routine lines, even one the cops had already covered or were covering, if it had offered any hope at all. We discussed all of them, and I made a list:

1. *Combing Rennert's apartment and Jane Ogilvy's cloister.*

2. *Trying to pry something out of Mrs. Jacobs and Mr. and Mrs. Ogilvy.*

3. *Getting the names of everybody who had known of the plan to go after Jacobs, analyzing them, and seeing those who were at all possible.*

4. *Trying to trace Jacobs to his meeting with X Monday evening, May 25th.*

5. *Trying to find someone who had seen a car parked in the lane back of the cloister Wednesday evening, May 27th.*

6. *Trying to find someone who had seen X, any stranger, entering the 37th Street building Wednesday night, May 27th.*

7. *Seeing a few hundred of the friends and associates of Jacobs, Jane Ogilvy, and Rennert, to find out if all three of them had been acquainted with a certain person or persons.*

8. *Trying to learn how Jacobs and Jane Ogilvy had disposed of the loot they got from Richard Echols and the estate of Marjorie Lippin; and supposing they had transferred a big share of it to X, trying to trace the transfers. Also the loot Alice Porter had got from Ellen Sturdevant.*

9. *Trying on Alice Porter the approach we had meant to try on Jane Ogilvy. Or trying to*

*throw a scare into her. Or trying to get from
Ellen Sturdevant and her publishers, McMurray & Co., an agreement not to prosecute or
demand repayment if Alice Porter would iden-
tify X.*

*10. Get a membership list of the NAAD and go
over it, name by name, with Cora Ballard.*

*11. Have a couple of hundred copies made of
"There Is Only Love," "What's Mine Is Yours,"
and "On Earth but Not in Heaven," and send
them to editors and book reviewers, with a letter citing the internal evidence that they had
all been written by the same person, and asking if they knew of any published material, or,
with editors, submitted material, apparently
by that person.*

During the discussion of this last item Wolfe had
before him the manuscripts of the first two, and the
copy of the third, they having been returned by
Cramer Friday afternoon as agreed.

There were other suggestions that I didn't bother
to put down. To each of the items listed I could have
added the objections and difficulties, but they're so obvious, especially to the routine ones, the first eight,
that I didn't think it was necessary.

The stymie was the motive. In ninety-nine murder
investigations out of a hundred it gets narrowed down
before long to just a few people who had motives,
often only two or three, and you go on from there. This
time the motive had been out in full view from the
start; the trouble was, who had it? It could be anyone
within reach who could read and write and drive a car
—say five million in the metropolitan area, and except

for Alice Porter there was absolutely no pointer. She was still alive at midnight Sunday. Orrie Cather, phoning from Carmel at 12:23 to report that Saul Panzer had relieved him on schedule, said that the light in the house had gone out at 10:52 and all had been quiet since. Wolfe had gone up to bed, leaving it that we would decide in the morning how to tackle Alice Porter.

In the kitchen at a quarter to nine Monday morning, as I was pouring a third cup of coffee, Fritz asked me what I was nervous about. I said I wasn't nervous. He said of course I was, I had been jerky for the last ten minutes, and I was taking a third cup of coffee. I said everybody in that house was too damned observant. He said, "See? You're very nervous"—and I took the coffee to the office.

I *was* nervous. Fred Durkin had phoned at 7:39 to say that he was on his way to relieve Saul, and Dol Bonner was with him, and Saul should have phoned by 8:20 to report, certainly not later than 8:30, and he hadn't. He still hadn't at 8:45. If it had been Fred or Orrie I would have thought it was probably some little snag like a flat tire, but Saul has never had a flat tire and never will. At nine o'clock I was sure there was some kind of hell to pay. At 9:15 I was sure that Alice Porter was dead. At 9:20 I was sure that Saul was dead too. When the phone rang at 9:25 I grabbed it and barked at it, "Well?"—which is no way to answer a phone.

"Archie?"

"Yes."

"Saul. We've got a circus up here."

I was so relieved to hear that all he had was a circus that I grinned at him. "You don't say. Did you get bit by a lion?"

"No. I got bit by a deputy sheriff and a state cop. Fred didn't show, and at eight-fifteen I went to where my car was hid. He was there, refusing to answer questions being asked by a deputy sheriff of Putnam County. Standing by was an old friend of yours, Sergeant Purley Stebbins."

"Oh. Ah."

"Yeah. Stebbins told the DS that I was another one of Nero Wolfe's operatives. That's all Stebbins said the whole time. He was leaving it to the DS, who said plenty. Evidently Fred had shown his driving license and then clammed. I thought that was a little extreme, especially with Stebbins there, and I supplied some essential details, but that didn't help any. The DS took both of us for trespassing and loitering, and then he added disturbing the peace. He used the radio in his car, and pretty soon a state cop came. On that dirt road it was a traffic jam. The state cop brought us to Carmel, and we are being held. This is my phone call to my lawyer. Apparently the DS is going to loiter near that house, and maybe Stebbins is too. On the way here we stopped for a couple of minutes on the blacktop where another state car was parked behind Dol Bonner's car at the roadside. Where she had had it behind some trees I suppose she was trespassing. She and a state cop were standing there chatting. If they have brought her on to Carmel I haven't seen her. I'm talking from a booth in the building where the sheriff's office is. The number of the sheriff's office is Carmel five-three-four-six-six."

When Saul makes a report there is nothing left to ask about. I asked. "Have you had any breakfast?"

"Not yet. I wanted to get you first. I will now."

"Eat plenty of meat. We'll try to spring you by the

Fourth of July. By the way, did you see Alice Porter before you left?"

"Sure. She was mowing the lawn."

I said that was fine, hung up, sat for two minutes looking at it, went to the stairs and mounted three flights to the plant rooms, and entered. At that point there were ten thousand orchid plants between me and my goal, many of them in full bloom, and the dazzle was enough to stop anyone, even one who had seen it as often as I had, but I kept going—through the first room, the moderate, then the tropical, and then the cool—on into the potting room. Theodore was at the sink, washing pots. Wolfe was at the big bench, putting peat mixture into flasks. When he heard my step and turned, his lips tightened and his chin went up. He knew I wouldn't mount three flights and burst in there for anything trivial.

"Relax," I said. "She's still alive, or was two hours ago. Mowing the lawn. But Saul and Fred are in the hoosegow, and Dol Bonner is having an affair with a state cop."

He turned to put the flask he was holding on the bench, and turned back. "Go on."

I did so, repeating verbatim what Saul and I had said. His chin went back to normal, but his lips stayed tight. When I finished he said, "So you regard my giving up meat as a subject for jest."

"I do not. I was being bitter."

"I know you. That deputy sheriff is probably an oaf. Have you phoned Mr. Parker?"

"No."

"Do so at once. Tell him to get those absurd charges dismissed if possible; if not, arrange for bail. And phone Mr. Harvey or Miss Ballard or Mr. Tabb that I shall be at that meeting at half past two."

I started. "What?"

"Must I repeat it?"

"No. Do you want me along?"

"Certainly."

I was thinking, as I returned down the aisles between the benches of orchids and on down the stairs, that this thing was going to set a record for smashing rules before we were through with it—if we ever got through. At my desk I rang the office of Nathaniel Parker, the lawyer Wolfe always uses when only a lawyer will do, and found him in. He didn't like the picture. He said rural communities resented having New York private detectives snooping around, especially when the snoopee was a property-owner and not a known criminal, and they weren't fond of New York lawyers either. He thought it would be better for him to relay the job to an attorney in Carmel whom he knew, instead of going up there himself, and I told him to go ahead. Another five Cs down the drain, at least.

I started to dial Philip Harvey's number but remembered in time that I had promised never to call him before noon except for an emergency, and dialed Jerome Tabb's instead. A female voice told me that Mr. Tabb was working and couldn't be disturbed until one o'clock, and would I leave a message. She seemed surprised and a little indignant that there was anyone on earth who didn't know that. I told her to tell him that Nero Wolfe would come to the council meeting at two-thirty, but, knowing that messages aren't always delivered, I got Cora Ballard at the NAAD office. She was delighted to hear that Wolfe would be present. I made two more calls, to Orrie Cather at home and to Sally Corbett at Dol Bonner's office, informing them about the circus and telling them the operation was off until further notice. Orrie, who was a free-lance, wanted to know if he was free to lance, and I told him no, to stand by. What the hell, another forty bucks was peanuts.

When I went to the kitchen to tell Fritz that lunch would be at one o'clock sharp because we were leaving at two for an appointment, he had a question. For Wolfe he was going to make a special omelet which he had just invented in his head, and would that do for me or should he broil some ham? I asked what would be in the omelet, and he said four eggs, salt, pepper, one tablespoon tarragon butter, two tablespoons cream, two tablespoons dry white wine, one-half teaspoon minced shallots, one-third cup whole almonds, and twenty fresh mushrooms. I thought that would do for two, but he said my God, no, that would be for Mr. Wolfe, and did I want one like it? I did. He warned me that he might decide at the last minute to fold some apricot jam in, and I said I would risk it.

Chapter 15

At 2:35 p.m. Wolfe and I, both of us well fueled with omelet, stepped out of a wobbly old elevator on the third floor of the Clover Club, which is in the Sixties just off Fifth Avenue. The hall was spacious and high-ceilinged and looked its age, but not much the worse for it. There was no one in sight. We glanced around, heard voices beyond a closed door, crossed to it, opened it, and entered.

Some three dozen people, all but six of them men, were seated around a long rectangular table covered with a white cloth. There were coffee cups, water glasses, ashtrays, pads of paper, and pencils. We stood, Wolfe with his hat in one hand and his cane in the other. Three or four of them were talking at once, and no one paid any attention to us. At the right end of the table were three of the committee members: Amy Wynn, Philip Harvey, and Mortimer Oshin. At the other end was Cora Ballard, and next to her was the president of the NAAD, Jerome Tabb. His picture had been on the jacket of his book I had read. Next to Tabb was the vice-president, a man who, according to an article I had read recently, averaged a million dollars a year from the musicals for which he had written the

books and lyrics. I had recognized some other faces—
four novelists, three dramatists, and a biographer or
something—by the time Harvey got up and came over
to us. The talk stopped, and heads were turned our
way.

"Nero Wolfe," Harvey told them. "Archie Goodwin."

He took Wolfe's hat and cane. An author or dramatist went and got two chairs and moved them near the
table. If I had been the president or the executive secretary the chairs would have been in place; after all,
we were expected.

As we sat, Jerome Tabb raised his voice. "You're a
little early, Mr. Wolfe." He glanced at his wrist. "It's
the time agreed, I know, but we haven't finished our
discussion."

"A sentry in the hall could have stopped us." Wolfe
was gruff. He always was when he had put his fanny
on a chair seat that was too small. "If the discussion
doesn't concern me you can finish it after I leave. If it
does concern me, proceed."

A famous woman novelist tittered, and two men
laughed. A famous dramatist said, "Let's hear what he
has to say. Why not?" A man raised his hand. "Mr.
President! As I said before, this is very irregular. We
almost never admit outsiders to a council meeting, and
I see no reason for making this an exception. The
chairman of the Joint Committee on Plagiarism has
reported and made a recommendation, and that should
be the basis of our . . ." He finished his sentence, but
I didn't catch it because five or six other voices
drowned him out.

Tabb tapped on a glass with a spoon, and the voices
subsided. "Having Mr. Wolfe here has been decided,"
he said with authority. "I told you he had been invited,

and a motion was made and seconded to admit him and hear him, and it carried by a voice vote. We won't go into that again. And I don't see how we can take a position based solely on the report and recommendation of the chairman of the joint committee. One reason we had to call this special meeting was that the three NAAD members of the committee don't agree. They actively disagree. I'm going to ask Mr. Wolfe to state his case, but first he ought to know in a general way how our discussion has gone. Now there shouldn't be any interruptions. Mr. Harvey, you first. Briefly."

The committee chairman cleared his throat. He looked around. "I've told you how I feel," he said. "I was never enthusiastic about hiring a private detective, but I went along with the majority of the committee. Now this matter has gone far beyond the province of the committee, what it was set up for. Three people have been killed. Nero Wolfe told the committee last week, last Wednesday, that he was going to expose the murderer of Simon Jacobs whether we terminated our engagement with him or not. Now I suppose he's going to expose the murderer of Jane Ogilvy and Kenneth Rennert. All right, that's fine, I'm all for exposing murderers, but that's not the job of this committee. It's not only not our job it's probably illegal and it could get us into serious trouble. We have no control over what Nero Wolfe does. He said he would have to have a free hand, that he wouldn't tell us what he was doing or was going to do. I say that's dangerous. As I said before, if the council doesn't instruct the committee to terminate the engagement with Nero Wolfe, the only thing I can do is resign from the committee. The way I feel, I'll have to."

Two or three of them started to say something, but

Tabb tapped on the glass. "You'll all get a chance later. Mr. Oshin? Briefly."

Oshin squashed a cigarette in an ashtray. "I'm in a different position now," he said, "now that Kenneth Rennert's dead. Before today I could be accused of having a personal interest, and I did. I don't deny that when I kicked in ten thousand dollars it was chiefly because I thought it might save me paying Rennert ten times that. Now personally I'm out from under. My ten thousand was a contribution to the expenses of the committee, and one of the publisher members, Dexter, has said he'll contribute whatever is necessary, and I think we should tell Nero Wolfe to go ahead. If we don't we're quitters. If he wants to expose a murderer, all right, if he exposes a murderer he will also expose the man that has been back of this plagiarism racket, and that's what we hired him for. *He* hasn't been murdered, he's still alive and still loose, and are we going to back out just because we've found out that he's not only a racketeer but a killer? I don't like threats to resign, I never have, but if you instruct the committee to fire Nero Wolfe I'll *have* to resign, and I wish I could resign from the NAAD too."

There were murmurs, and Tabb tapped on the glass again. "Miss Wynn? Briefly, please."

Amy Wynn's nose had been twitching. Her clasped hands were resting on the edge of the table. She was up against it, since Reuben Imhof wasn't there for her to look at. "I really don't think," she said, "that I should take a position on this. Because I'm in the same—"

"Louder, Miss Wynn, please."

She raised her voice a little. "I'm in the same position that Mr. Oshin was. The man that made the claim against him is dead, but the woman that has made a

claim against me, Alice Porter, is still alive. Nero
Wolfe says that my case is different, that the story she
bases her claim on wasn't written by the man who
wrote the others, that Alice Porter wrote it herself,
but that doesn't really matter, because he wrote the
story that she used for her claim against Ellen Sturdevant, so if he's caught and it all comes out she'll be
caught too, and I'll be out from under too, as Mr. Oshin
put it. So I still have a personal interest, a strong personal interest, and I don't think I should take a position. Perhaps I shouldn't be on the committee. I'll
resign if you think I ought to."

"Damn fine committee," someone muttered.
"They're *all* going to resign." Harvey started to speak,
but Tabb tapped on the glass. "We're not through," he
said. "I'm going to ask our counsel to say a word about
Mr. Harvey's statement that it's probably illegal for us
to continue the arrangement with Mr. Wolfe and it
might get us into serious trouble. Mr. Sachs?"

A compact, broad-shouldered guy about my age
with sharp dark eyes passed his tongue over his lips.
"It's not a very complicated situation legally," he said.
"There should be a letter to Mr. Wolfe stating defi-
nitely and specifically that you have engaged him to
investigate the plagiarism claims and nothing else.
Then if he does something that causes him to be
charged with some offense against the law, for instance withholding evidence or obstructing justice, no
matter what, you wouldn't be liable legally. Of course
there could be bad publicity, there might be a stigma
because you had hired him, but it's not actionable to
hire a man who breaks a law while he is in your employ unless his offense is committed under your direction or with your knowledge and consent. If you decide

to send such a letter I'll be glad to draft it if you want me to."

Wolfe and I exchanged glances. He sounded exactly like Nathaniel Parker. Tabb spoke. "Apparently that settles that. I'm going to ask Miss Ballard what she thinks. She tried a couple of times to tell us, but we didn't let her finish. Cora? Briefly."

The executive secretary looked apologetic. She was tapping on a pad with her pencil. "I don't know," she said, "I guess the fact is I'm just afraid. I know Mr. Wolfe is a very brilliant man, I know a little bit about how he does things, I suppose you all do, and of course I'm not going to criticize him, he knows his business just as you know your business of writing, but I'd hate to have the association get involved in something sensational like a murder trial. One thing Mr. Harvey didn't say, the New York police are working on this now, and since there have been three murders I think you can be pretty sure they won't quit until they get the man they're after, and since he's the man we're after too I shouldn't think you'd have to pay a private detective to do what they're doing." She smiled apologetically. "I hope Mr. Oshin won't mind if I don't agree that you would be quitters."

"I don't agree either," Philip Harvey blurted. "I don't see how we could be expected—"

Tabb was tapping on the glass. Harvey was going on anyhow, but several of them shushed him. "I think we've covered the various viewpoints pretty well," Tabb said. "Mr. Wolfe? If you care to comment?"

Wolfe's head went from right to left and back again. Those with their backs to us twisted around on their chairs. "First," he said, "I remark that with your books two of you have given me pleasure, three of you have informed me, and one of you has stimulated my mental processes. Two or—"

"Name them," the famous woman novelist demanded.

Laughter. Tabb tapped on the glass.

Wolfe resumed. "Two or three of you have irritated or bored me, but on balance I owe you much. That's why I'm here. Having seen your names on the letterhead of your association, I wanted to prevent you from forsaking a responsibility. You are collectively responsible for the death by violence of three people."

Five or six of them spoke at once. Tabb didn't tap on the glass. Wolfe showed them a palm. "If you please. I merely stated a fact. You appointed a committee for a specific purpose. Pursuant to that purpose, the committee hired me to investigate. It provided me with the record—various documents and other material. Studying it, I formed a conclusion that should have been reached long ago: that the three first claims of plagiarism had all been instigated by a single person. I procured more material, books written by the claimants, and formed a second conclusion: that none of the three claimants had been the instigator. That changed completely the character of the investigation. It widened its scope so greatly that I told the committee it was no longer my kind of job. It was a member of the committee who suggested a plan to beguile one of the claimants, Simon Jacobs, into turning informer. At the request of the committee, reluctantly, I agreed to carry out the plan, which by its nature had to be imparted to various people. Forty-seven persons knew of it within a few hours. As a direct result of the plan Simon Jacobs was killed before Mr. Goodwin got to him; and as a further direct result, because the man we were after feared that a similar plan would be tried on

Jane Ogilvy or Kenneth Rennert, they too were killed."

Wolfe's head went left and right again. "I repeat that the conclusions I formed should have been reached long ago, if a competent investigation had been made. The evidence on which they were based had been at hand, all of it, for more than a year. Because of those conclusions, formed in my pursuit of the stated purpose of the committee, and because of a plan of procedure approved by your committee and suggested by one of its members, Mr. Oshin, three people were killed. You are now considering whether or not to scuttle. That might be prudent; certainly it would not be gallant; some might think it less than honorable. I submit it to your judgment. Mr. Harvey. Do you challenge any of my facts?"

"Your facts are straight enough," Harvey conceded, "but you left one out. You told us yourself that you failed to function properly. You admitted that but for your default Jacobs would still be alive. Are we responsible for your blunder?"

"No." Wolfe was blunt. "With the plan known to so many, I should have taken precautions to safeguard Mr. Jacobs from harm. But you have shifted your ground. My default does not relieve this body of its responsibility. If you wish to dismiss me for incompetence I offer no objection, but then, to honor your obligation, you'll have to hire somebody else. Mr. Tabb. You invited my comments and I have made them." He stood up. "If that's all—"

"Wait a minute." Tabb's eyes moved. "Do you want to ask Mr. Wolfe any questions?"

"I have one," a man said. "Mr. Wolfe, you heard Mr. Sachs's suggestion, that we write you a letter saying that you are to investigate the plagiarism claims and nothing else. Would you accept such a letter?"

"Certainly. If I get the swindler, which will satisfy you, I'll also get the murderer, which will satisfy me."

"Then I make a motion. I move that we instruct the chairman of the committee to ask Mr. Sachs to draft the letter, and sign it and send it to Nero Wolfe, and tell him to go ahead with the investigation."

Two of them, a man and a woman, seconded it.

"You understand," Harvey said, "that I couldn't obey those instructions. If the motion passes you'll have to get a new chairman."

"Mortimer Oshin," someone said.

"That will come after we act on the motion," Tabb said. "Or it won't. Before we discuss it, have you any more questions for Mr. Wolfe?"

"I'd like to ask him," a woman said, "if he knows who the murderer is."

Wolfe, on his feet, grunted. "If I did I wouldn't be here."

"Any further questions?" Tabb asked. Apparently not. "Then discussion of the motion."

"You don't need us for that," Wolfe said. "I appreciate the courtesy of your invitation to be present, and if my opening remark gave you the impression that I accepted it solely to prevent you from forsaking a responsibility I wish to correct it. I also wish to earn a fee. Come, Archie."

He wheeled and headed for the door, and I circled around him to open it, detouring to get his hat and cane from a chair.

Chapter 16

We got home at 3:55, just in the nick of time for Wolfe to keep his afternoon date with the orchids. On my desk were three memos from Fritz, reporting phone calls—one from Lon Cohen, one from Dexter of Title House, and one from a personal friend. I rang Dexter. He wanted to know if there was any truth in the rumor that the NAAD council was holding a special meeting for the purpose of instructing the joint committee to terminate its engagement with Wolfe. Thinking it would be unwise to tell a publisher, even one with a conscience, what authors and dramatists had done or were doing, I said we had heard the rumor but knew nothing definite, which was true, since we hadn't stayed for the vote on the motion. He said if the NAAD council didn't know that they couldn't give orders to a *joint* committee they would soon find out. I didn't bother with Lon Cohen; he could ring again. The personal friend was a personal matter, and I attended to it.

A little after five Saul Panzer called, from a booth in a Carmel drugstore. "We've been liberated," he said. "Free as crows. No charges. The lawyer is at the fountain with Miss Bonner and Fred, having a milk-shake. Now what?"

"No program," I told him. "I don't suppose there's any chance of keeping on her?"

"I doubt it. I don't see how. I just got back from a little ride out that way. There's a car there in the same spot we've been using, I suppose a deputy sheriff's. He's probably covering the house. Also there's a car near the spot Miss Bonner and Miss Corbett were using, with a man in it. It looks as if Stebbins has fed Putnam County a line. About the only way would be to come in from the back, walk in about a mile from another road to a hill with trees on it, and use binoculars. Five hundred yards from the house. Of course that would be no good after dark."

I said it wouldn't be much better even before dark and told him to go home and get some sleep and stand by, and the same for Fred. Also to tell Dol Bonner she would hear from us when we had anything to say. Two minutes after I hung up the phone rang again.

"Nero Wolfe's office, Archie Goodwin speaking."

"This is the chairman of the Joint Committee on Plagiarism. You may recognize my voice."

"I do. Was it a close vote?"

"We don't reveal details of our deliberations to outsiders, but it wasn't close. The letter has been drafted and you'll have it tomorrow. I don't ask you what the next move is, since Wolfe doesn't reveal details either, but I thought he'd like to know that we're both gallant and honorable. Sometimes."

"He will, Mr. Oshin. Congratulations. Who's the new committee member?"

"Oh, Harvey's still on the committee. He only re-signed as chairman. I think he wants to keep his eye on us. Let me know if you need a bat boy."

I said I would.

When Wolfe came down at six o'clock I reported the calls to him—Dexter and Saul and Oshin. As I finished, Fritz entered with a tray—a bottle of beer and a glass. Wolfe glared at him, and he stopped halfway to the desk.

"Archie put you up to this," Wolfe said coldly.

"No, sir. I thought perhaps—"

"Take it back. I am committed. Take it back!"

Fritz went. Wolfe transferred the glare to me. "Is Alice Porter still alive?"

"I don't know. Saul saw her at eight this morning, ten hours ago."

"I want to see her. Bring her."

"Now?"

"Yes."

I regarded him. "Some day," I said, "you're going to tell me to bring you the Queen of England, and I'll do my best. But I remind you that two or three times, when you have told me to bring someone and I have done so, you didn't like the method I used. Do you want to suggest one this time?"

"Yes. Tell her that I am ready to make a settlement with her for her claim against Amy Wynn."

I raised a brow. "What if she wants to know what kind of a settlement?"

"You don't know. You only know that I am ready to make one, and tomorrow may be too late."

"What if she phones Amy Wynn and learns that you haven't been told to make a settlement?"

"That's why you're going after her instead of phoning. She probably won't; but if she does you'll say that I am not making the offer on behalf of Miss Wynn. I am making it on behalf of my client, the committee. I would prefer not to have that said unless it's necessary."

"Okay." I got up. "Would it help if I had some idea of what you *are* going to say to her?"

"No. It only occurred to me as I was coming down in the elevator. It should have occurred to me long ago. I am beginning to suspect that my mind is going. It should have occurred to you. A screw to use on that woman has been staring us in the face for a full week, and neither of us had the wit to see it. Now that I've told you it's there, of course you will."

But I didn't. I had plenty of time to try to, going to the garage to get the car, and then a ninety-minute drive, but I simply couldn't see it. You probably have, and if not you will now if you spend three minutes looking for it, and of course you'll think I'm as dumb as they come, but you've had it all in one package while with me it had been dragging along for two weeks and a lot of things had been on my mind, including three murders. Anyhow, dumb or not, I didn't hit on it until just as I was turning off of Route 301 onto the blacktop. Then, suddenly seeing it, I braked the car, steered it onto the grass shoulder, stopped, and sat looking it over. No wonder Wolfe had suspected his mind was going. It was perfectly obvious. I fed gas, eased back onto the road, and went on. We had her.

But I had to get her first. If X had got there ahead of me and stuck a knife in her, I would reverse my stand on boiled cucumbers; I would eat nothing *but* boiled cucumbers until we nailed him. I had intended to take it easy along the stretch of blacktop and see if I could spot the man in the car near the place Dol Bonner and Sally Corbett had used, but now I was in a hurry. Almost too much of a hurry; I wasn't careful enough on the half-mile of narrow winding dirt road and scraped my bottom on a high center. That's no way to treat a Heron sedan. Slowing down, I turned into the lane through the gap and bumped along the ruts to the little blue house. It was ten minutes past eight, and the sun was just sinking behind the rim of a ridge.

I had seen her before I stopped the car. She was a couple of hundred yards off to the left, standing by a stone fence. The bicolored mutt was there beside her, wagging his tail, and on the other side of the fence was the upper half of a man. Her raised voice came across the meadow. I got out and headed for them, and as I approached I could hear her words: ". . . and you can tell the sheriff I don't need any protection and don't want any! You get out of here and stay out! I'm not in any danger, and if I am I can handle it! I told that state trooper this morning that I don't want—"

The man's eyes left her to come to me, and she whirled around. "You here again?" she demanded.

I stopped at the fence and addressed the man on the other side. "Trespassing and loitering," I said sternly. "Also disturbing the peace. A peeping Tom can get up to three years. Beat it."

"You too," Alice Porter said. "Both of you beat it."

"I'm an officer of the law," the man said, raising a hand to exhibit a medal. "Deputy Sheriff Putnam County."

Everyone glared at everyone. "Tell Sergeant Stebbins," I instructed the man, "that Archie Goodwin was here. It will please him." I turned to her. "When I saw you ten days ago you said you wouldn't talk, not a word, and evidently you haven't changed your mind. But you also said you'd listen if I had come to make an offer. Okay, I have one."

"What kind of an offer?"

"It's just for you. I doubt if the deputy sheriff would be interested."

When she looked straight at you her eyes seemed even closer together, and her little nose almost wasn't there. "All right," she said, "I'll listen." She told the man, "You clear out of here and stay out." She turned and headed for the house.

It was a procession across the meadow. First her, then the dog, then me; and what made it a procession was the deputy sheriff, who climbed the wall and tagged along behind, ten paces back of me. She didn't look back until she reached the door of the house; then she saw him. He had stopped at my car and opened the door on the other side, the driver's side. "That's all right," I told her, "let him inspect it. He needs something to do." When she opened the door the dog trotted in, and I followed.

It was a bigger room than you would expect from the outside, and wasn't bad at all. She said, "Sit down if you want to," and went and deposited her 160 pounds on a long wicker bench. I pulled a chair around. "What kind of an offer?" she asked.

I sat. "I haven't actually got it, Miss Porter. Nero Wolfe has it. If you'll come with me to his house in New York he'll tell you about it. It's an offer to settle your claim against Amy Wynn."

"An offer from her?"

"I don't know all the details, but I think so."

"Then you think wrong."

"I often do. That's just the impression I got. It could be that Mr. Wolfe wants to make an offer on behalf of his client, the Joint Committee on Plagiarism of the National Association of Authors and Dramatists and the Book Publishers of America. But I think it's from Amy Wynn."

"You're not very good at thinking. You'd better stop trying. I'm not going to New York to see Nero Wolfe. If he really has an offer and you don't know what it is, call him on the phone and ask him. There's the phone. Reverse the charges."

She meant it. I had crossed my legs. Now I uncrossed them. Since the method Wolfe had suggested wouldn't work, I would have to roll my own. "Look, Miss Porter. I drove all the way up here instead of phoning because I thought your line might be tapped. Why has that deputy sheriff been hiding behind that stone fence all day? Why is another one in a car hiding behind some bushes near the road a mile from here? Why did a state cop come to see you this morning? Who started all the fuss? I can tell you. A man named Purley Stebbins of the New York police. He's a sergeant on the Manhattan West Homicide Squad. He's investigating three murders that have taken place in the past two weeks that you have probably heard about. That man out there said he's here to protect you. Blah. He's here to see that you don't skip. We'll be followed when we drive to New York, see if we're not. I don't—"

"I'm not going to New York."

"You're a damn fool if you don't. I don't know what Stebbins has on you for the murders, but he must have something, or thinks he has, or he wouldn't have come up here and sicked Putnam County on you. I'm telling the truth when I say that Nero Wolfe didn't tell me exactly why he wants to see you, and see you quick, but I know this, he doesn't suspect you of murder."

"You said he wants to make me an offer."

"Maybe he does. He said to tell you that. All I know is this, if I were in any way connected with a murder, let alone three murders, and if Nero Wolfe was investigating them, and if he wanted to see me and said it was urgent, and if I was innocent, I wouldn't sit around arguing about it."

"I'm not connected with any murder." She was hooked; I could see it in her eyes.

"Good. Tell Sergeant Stebbins that." I left the chair. "He'll be glad to know it. I apologize for butting in on your talk with your protector." I turned and was going, and was halfway to the door when her voice came.

"Wait a minute."

I stood. She was biting her lip. She wasn't looking at me, but here and there. Finally she focused on me. "If I go with you, how will I get home? I could take my car, but I don't like to drive at night."

"I'll bring you home."

She arose. "I'll put on a dress. Go out and tell that damn deputy sheriff to go soak his head."

I went out, but I didn't deliver the message. The officer of the law wasn't in sight at first glance, but then I saw him, across the meadow by the stone fence, and there were two of him. Apparently it was an around-the-clock cover, and his relief had come. To show there was no hard feeling I waved at them, but they didn't wave back. I got the car turned around, looked in the trunk to see that my emergency kit was still there, and checked the contents of the dash compartment, and pretty soon Alice Porter emerged, locked the door, patted the dog, and came and got in. The dog escorted us through the gap to the dirt road and then let us go.

I stayed under thirty on the blacktop to give anyone who might be interested time to see that she was in the car with me, and to get out to the road and fall in, and when I stopped at the junction with Route 301

I picked him up in the mirror, but I didn't call Alice Porter's attention to him until we were the other side of Carmel and I was sure it was a tail. It's fun to drop a tail, but it would help to put her in a proper mood for conversation with Wolfe if he stuck all the way, so I made no difficulties. She twisted around in the seat about every four minutes for a look back, and by the time we rolled into the garage on Tenth Avenue her neck must have needed a rest. I don't know if he got his car parked, and out of it, in time to stalk us a block to 35th Street and around the corner to the old brownstone.

I put her in the front room and showed her the door to the bathroom, and then, instead of using the connecting door to the office, went around by the hall. Wolfe, at his desk with a French magazine, looked up. "You got her?"

I nodded. "I thought I'd better report first. Her reaction seemed a little peculiar."

"How peculiar?"

I gave it to him verbatim. He took ten seconds to digest it and said, "Bring her." I went and opened the connecting door and said, "In here, Miss Porter." She had taken off her jacket, and either she didn't wear a bra or she needed a new one. Wolfe was on his feet; I have never understood why, considering how he feels about women, he bothers to stand when one enters the room. He waited until she was in the red leather chair, with her jacket draped over the arm, to resume his seat.

He eyed her. "Mr. Goodwin tells me," he said civilly, "that you and your home are well guarded."

She was forward in the chair, her elbows resting on the arms. "I don't need any guard," she said. "He got me to come here by trying to scare me about being suspected of murder. I don't scare easy. I'm not scared."

"But you came."

She nodded. "I'm here. I wanted to see what kind of a game this is. He talked about an offer, but I don't believe you've got an offer. What have you got?"

"You're wrong, Miss Porter." Wolfe leaned back, comfortable. "I do have an offer. I'm prepared to offer you easement from the threat of prosecution for an offense you have committed. Naturally I want something in return."

"Nobody's going to prosecute me. I haven't committed any offense."

"But you have." Wolfe stayed affable, not accusing, just stating a fact. "A serious one. A felony. Before I describe the offense I'm referring to, the one for which you will pay no penalty if you accept my offer, I must fill in some background. Four years ago, in nineteen fifty-five, you entered into a conspiracy with some person, to me unknown, to extort money from Ellen Sturdevant by making a false claim of plagiarism. It—"

"That's a lie."

"If so it's defamatory and you have me. The next year, nineteen fifty-six, that same person, call him X, entered into a similar conspiracy with a man named Simon Jacobs to defraud Richard Echols; and in nineteen fifty-seven he repeated the performance with a woman named Jane Ogilvy, to defraud Marjorie Lippin. All three of the conspiracies were successful; large sums were paid. Last year, nineteen fifty-eight, X tried it again, with a man named Kenneth Rennert; that time the target was a playwright, Mortimer Oshin. No settlement had been made at the time Rennert died, five days ago."

"It's probably all lies. The one about me is."

Wolfe ignored it. "I'm making this as brief as possible, including only what is essential for you to understand my offer. I learned of the existence of X by a textual study of the three stories that were the basis of the claims made by you, Simon Jacobs, and Jane Ogilvy. They were all written by the same person. That is demonstrable and beyond question. I communicated my discovery to seven people, perforce, and they passed it on. A plan was made to entice Simon Jacobs into revealing the identity of X, and it became known to some fifty persons. X learned of it, and he killed Simon Jacobs before we got to him; and, fearing that we would try some similar plan with Jane Ogilvy or Kenneth Rennert, he killed them also. I don't know why he hasn't killed you too. He or she."

"Why should he? I don't know any X. I wrote that story myself. 'There Is Only Love.'"

"If so you are X, and I have reason to believe that you are not." Wolfe shook his head. "No. Did you write that book that was published under your name? *The Moth That Ate Peanuts?*"

"Certainly I wrote it!"

"Then you didn't write that story. That too is demonstrable. And that is the background." Wolfe straightened up and flattened a palm on the desk. "Now. Here is the point. I have also studied the text of 'Opportunity Knocks,' the story on which you have based your claim against Amy Wynn. Did you write that?"

"Certainly I did!"

"I believe you. It was written by the person who wrote *The Moth That Ate Peanuts*. But in that case you did *not* write 'There Is Only Love.' I will undertake to establish that fact beyond a reasonable doubt to the satisfaction of both a learned judge and a motley jury; and if it can be demonstrated that your claim against Ellen Sturdevant was a fraud, that it was based on a story you did not write, how much credence will be given to your good faith in your claim against Amy Wynn? I am prepared to advise Miss Wynn to reject your claim out of hand."

"Go ahead." Evidently she had meant it when she said she didn't scare easy.

"You are not impressed?" Wolfe was still affable.

"I certainly am not. You're lying and you're bluffing —if I get what you're driving at. You think you can prove I didn't write that story, 'There Is Only Love,' by showing that its style is different from my book, *The Moth That Ate Peanuts.* Is that it?"

"Yes. If you include all the elements of style—vocabulary, syntax, paragraphing. Yes."

"I'd like to see you try." She was scornful. "Any writer that's any good can imitate a style. They do it all the time. Look at all the parodies."

Wolfe nodded. "Of course. There have been many masters of parody in the world's literature. But you're overlooking a vital point. As I said, the three stories that were the basis of the first three claims *were all written by the same person.* Or, if you prefer, put it that a comparison of their texts would convince any qualified student of writing, an experienced editor or writer, that they were written by the same person. You will either have to concede that or you will have to contend that when you wrote 'There Is Only Love' you either invented a style quite different from your normal style as in your book, or you parodied the style of someone else, call him Y; that when Simon Jacobs wrote 'What's Mine Is Yours' he parodied either Y or your story; and that when Jane Ogilvy wrote 'On

Earth but Not in Heaven' she parodied either Y, or your story, which had not been published, or Simon Jacobs' story, also unpublished. That is patently preposterous. If you offered that fantasy in a courtroom the jury wouldn't even leave the box. Do you still maintain that you wrote 'There Is Only Love'?"

"Yes." But her tone was different and so were her eyes. "I have never seen those stories by Simon Jacobs and Jane Ogilvy. I still say you're bluffing."

"I have them here. Archie. Get them. Including Miss Porter's."

I went and got them from the safe and handed them to her, and stood there.

"Take your time," Wolfe told her. "We have all night."

Hers was on top. She only glanced at it, the first page, and put it on the stand beside the chair. The next one was "What's Mine Is Yours," by Simon Jacobs. She read the first page and part of the second, and put it on top of hers on the stand. With "On Earth but Not in Heaven," by Jane Ogilvy, she finished the first page but didn't even glance at the second. As she put it down I circled around her chair to get them, but Wolfe told me to leave them, saying that she might want to inspect them further.

He regarded her. "So you know I'm not bluffing."

"I haven't said so."

"You have indicated it by your cursory examination of those manuscripts. Either study them as they deserve or yield the point."

"I'm not yielding anything. You said you have an offer. What is it?"

His tone sharpened. "First the threat. A double threat. There is good ground, I think, for Ellen Sturdevant to bring an action against you for libel and for recovery of the money she paid you. Legal points on the rules of evidence would be involved, and I am not a lawyer. But I am certain that Amy Wynn can successfully sue you for libel and can also have you charged with attempted extortion, a criminal offense."

"Let her try. She wouldn't dare."

"I think she would. Also I have read your letter to the Victory Press, in which you demanded payment from them as well as Amy Wynn. When I explain the situation to Mr. Imhof as I have explained it to you, I shall suggest that he take steps to have you charged with attempted extortion, either jointly with Miss Wynn or independently. I'm sure he won't hesitate. He resents the planting of the manuscript in his office."

She was impressed at last. She opened her mouth and closed it again. She swallowed. She bit her lip. Finally she spoke. "The manuscript wasn't planted."

"Really, Miss Porter." Wolfe shook his head. "If you have any wits at all you must know that won't do. Do you wish to examine those stories further?"

"No."

"Then take them, Archie."

I went and got them, put them in the safe, and closed the door. As I returned to my desk Wolfe was resuming. "So much for the threats. Now for the offer. One: I will not advise Ellen Sturdevant to bring an action against you. It's possible she will do so of her own accord, but I won't instigate it. Two: I will prevail upon Miss Wynn and Mr. Imhof to bring no action against you, either civil or criminal. I'm sure I can. Those are the two items of my part of the bargain. Your part also has two items. One: you will renounce your claim against Amy Wynn and the Victory Press, in writing. Not a confession of wrongdoing; merely a renunciation of the claim because it was made in error.

It will be drawn by a lawyer. Two: you will tell me X's name. That's all I ask; you need not—"

"I don't know any X."

"Pfui. You need not furnish any evidence or particulars; I'll get them myself. Nothing in writing; merely tell me his name and where to find him. I am not supposing that you know anything of his conspiracies with Simon Jacobs and Jane Ogilvy and Kenneth Rennert, or of his killing them; I am willing to assume your total ignorance of those events. Just tell me the name of the man or woman who wrote 'There Is Only Love.' "

"I wrote it."

"Nonsense. That won't do, Miss Porter."

"It will have to do." Her hands were in her lap, tightly clasped, and there was sweat on her forehead. "The other part, about the Victory Press and Amy Wynn, all right, I'll do that. If they'll sign a paper not to sue me or have me prosecuted or anything, I'll sign one giving up my claim because I made it in error. I still don't think you could prove what you said you could. Maybe you're not bluffing, but you can't prove anything just by showing there's something similar about the way those stories were written. If you want to think there's an X somewhere, I can't help that, but I can't tell you his name if I don't know anything about him."

I was focused on her. I wouldn't have supposed she was such a good liar. I was thinking that no matter how good you think you are at sizing people up, you can never be sure how well a certain specimen can do a certain thing until you see him try. Or her. I was also thinking that the screw we had thought would squeeze it out of her apparently wasn't going to work without more pressure, and how would Wolfe give it another turn? Evidently, since he wasn't speaking, he was asking the same question, and I moved my eyes to him.

And got a surprise. He not only wasn't speaking; he wasn't looking. He was leaning back with his eyes closed and his lips moving. He was pushing out his lips, puckered, and drawing them in—out and in, out and in. He only does that, and always does it, when he has found the crack he has been looking for, or thinks he has found it, and is trying to see through; and as I say, I was surprised. It shouldn't have been such a strain on his brain to figure out how to bear down on Alice Porter; he simply had to show her what she was in for if he made good on his threats. I looked back at her. She had got a handkerchief from her bag and was wiping her brow.

Wolfe opened his eyes, straightened up, and cocked his head. "Very well, Miss Porter," he said. "You can't tell me what you don't know, assuming that you really don't. I'll have to re-examine my conjectures and my conclusions. You'll hear from me again when I have conferred with Miss Wynn and Mr. Imhof. They will surely agree to the proposed arrangement. Mr. Goodwin will drive you home. Archie?"

So the strain on his brain had been something else, I had no idea what. Whenever that happens, when he goes off somewhere out of sight, I am not supposed to yodel at him, especially with company present, so I got to my feet and asked if there were any errands on the way, and he said no. Alice Porter was going to say something and decided not to. When I held her jacket she missed the armhole twice, and I admit it could have been partly my fault. My mind was occupied. It was starting back over the conversation, her part of it, trying to spot what had opened up a crack for Wolfe.

It was still trying three hours and twenty minutes

later, at half past two in the morning, when I mounted the stoop of the old brownstone and let myself in. At one point on the way back, as I was rolling along on the parkway, I had thought I had it. Alice Porter was X. When she had written the first one, "There Is Only Love," she had used another style, as different as she could make it from her own style in her book. But there were three things wrong with that. First, if she had been slick enough to make up a style for the first one, why hadn't she made up other styles for the other two instead of copying that one? Second, why had she used her own style for "Opportunity Knocks," the one she had used on Amy Wynn? Third, what had she said that gave Wolfe so strong a suspicion that she was X that he called a halt and started on his lip routine? I had to try again, and was still at it when I got home.

There was a note on my desk for me:

AG:

Saul, Fred, Orrie, Miss Bonner, and Miss Corbett will come at eight in the morning and come to my room. I have taken $1000 from the safe to give them for expenses. You will not be needed. You will of course sleep late.

NW

Wolfe has his rules and I have mine. I absolutely refuse to permit any wear and tear on my brain after my head hits the pillow. Usually it works automatically, but that night a little discipline was needed. It took me a full three minutes to fade out.

Chapter 17

In bed at three and out of it at ten Wednesday morning, I was an hour short of my regular requirement of eight hours' sleep, but with Wolfe working his lips and giving up on Alice Porter and arranging a before-breakfast session with the hired hands, all five of them, it looked as if we were getting set for a showdown, and in that case I should be willing to make a major personal sacrifice, so I rolled out at ten. Also I made it snappy showering and dressing and eating breakfast, and got to the office at 11:15, only a quarter of an hour after Wolfe got down from the plant rooms. He was at his desk with the morning mail. I went and sat and watched him slit envelopes. His hands are quick and accurate, and he would be good at manual labor provided he could do it sitting down. I asked if he wanted help and he said no. I asked if there were any instructions.

"Perhaps." He quit slitting and looked up. "After we discuss a matter."

"Good. I guess I'm awake enough to discuss if it's not too complicated. First I'll report my conversation with Alice Porter during our drive to Carmel. At one point she said, 'I never drive at night on account of my eyes. It gives me a headache.' That's the crop. Not another word. I made no advances because after the way you suddenly quit on her I had no idea where to poke. Next, it wouldn't hurt if I had some notion of what Saul and Fred and Orrie and Dol Bonner and Sally Corbett are up to. So that when they call in I'll know what they're talking about."

"They'll report to me."

"I see. Like that again. What I don't know won't hurt you."

"What you don't know will make no demands on your powers of dissimulation." He put the letter-opener down. It was a knife with a horn handle that had been thrown at him in 1954, in the cellar of an old border fort in Alabama, by a man named Bua. The Marley .38 with which I had shot Bua was in a drawer of my desk. He continued, "Besides, you won't be here. I have made an assumption which was prompted by the question, why is Alice Porter alive? Why did X remove the other three so expeditiously and make no attempt to remove her? And why is she so cocksure that she is in no danger? Alone in that secluded house, with no companion but a dog that dotes on strangers, she shows no trepidation whatever, though X could be lurking at her door or behind a bush by day or by night. Why?"

I flipped a hand. "Any one of a dozen reasons. The best is the simplest. Also it's been done so often that she wouldn't have to invent it. She wrote a detailed account of how she and X put the bite on Ellen Sturdevant, probably saying it was X's idea, and put it in an envelope. She also put in the envelope things that would corroborate it, for instance something in X's handwriting, maybe a couple of letters he had written her; that would make it better. She sealed the envelope thoroughly with wax and tape, and wrote on it, 'To be opened on my death and not before,' and signed it. Then she deposited it with somebody she was sure she could trust to follow the instructions, and she told X about it, probably sending him or giving him a copy of what she had written. So X was up a stump. It was done first about three thousand B.C., and maybe a million times since, but it still works. It has saved the lives of thousands of blackmailers, and also of a lot of fine citizens like Alice Porter." I flipped a hand again. "I like that best, but of course there are others."

He grunted. "That one will do. That's the assumption I have made. I think it highly probable. So where is the envelope?"

I raised a brow. "Probably somewhere in the United States, and there are now fifty of them. I doubt if she sent it out of the country. Do you want me to find it?"

"Yes."

I got up. "Are you in a hurry?"

"Don't clown. If such an envelope exists, and I strongly suspect that it does, I want to know where it is. If we can get our hands on it, all the better, but merely to locate it would be enough. Where would you start?"

"I'd have to think it over. Her bank, her lawyer if she has one, her pastor if she goes to church, a relative or an intimate friend—"

"Much too diffuse. It would take days. You might get a hint, or even better than a hint, from the executive secretary, Cora Ballard. Alice Porter joined that association in nineteen fifty-one, was dropped for nonpayment of dues in nineteen fifty-four, and rejoined in nineteen fifty-six. I gathered that Miss Ballard is extremely well informed about the members, and presumably she will help if she can. See her."

"Okay. She may not be enthusiastic. She wanted them to fire you. But I suppose she'll—"

The doorbell rang. I stepped to the hall, took a look through the one-way glass panel, and turned to tell Wolfe, "Cramer." He made a face and growled, "I have nothing for him." I asked if I should tell him that and ask him to come back tomorrow, and he said yes, and then said, "Confound it, he'll be after me all day and you won't be here. Let him in."

I went to the front and opened the door and got a shock, or rather, a series of shocks. Cramer said, "Good morning," distinctly, as he crossed the threshold, plainly implying that I was a fellow being. Then he dropped his hat on the bench and waited while I closed the door, instead of tramping on to the office. Then he not only told Wolfe good morning but asked him how he was. Evidently it was Brotherhood Day. I had to control an impulse to slap him on the back or poke him in the ribs. To cap it, he said as he sat in the red leather chair, "I hope you won't be charging me rent for this chair." Wolfe said politely that a guest was always welcome to a seat to rest his legs, and Cramer said, "And a glass of beer?"

It was a ticklish situation. If Wolfe pushed the button, the beer signal, two shorts and a long, Fritz would get a wrong impression and there would have to be an explanation. He looked at me, and I got up and went to the kitchen, got a tray and a bottle and a glass, telling Fritz it was for a guest, and returned. As I entered Cramer was saying, ". . . but I never expected to see the day when you would cut down on your beer. What next? Thank you, Goodwin." He poured. "What I'm here for, I came to apologize. One day last week—

Friday, I think it was—I accused you of using Jane
Ogilvy for a decoy and bungling it. I may have been
wrong. If you or Goodwin told anybody you were going after her he's not admitting it. And Kenneth Rennert was killed that same night, and you certainly
wouldn't have set them both up. So I owe you an apology." He picked up the glass and drank.

"It's welcome," Wolfe told him. "All the more since
you owe me a dozen other apologies that you have
never made. Let this one do for all."

"You're so goddam impervious." Cramer put the
glass down on the stand. "Instead of coming to apologize, I could have come to tell you to stop interfering
with a homicide investigation. You sent Goodwin to
Putnam County to coerce a woman into coming to see
you, a woman who was under surveillance by officers
of the law."

"Possibly you did."

"Did what?"

"Come for that purpose. There was no coercion."

"The hell there wasn't. She went to the sheriff's
office in Carmel this morning and told him to keep his
men away from her place, and she said that Goodwin
had told her that Sergeant Stebbins had sicked Putnam County on her because he suspected her of murder, and she had better go with him to see you, and go
quick. That's not coercion?" He looked at me. "Did you
tell her that?"

"Sure I did. Why not? Have you crossed her off?"

"No." He went to Wolfe. "He admits it. I call that
interfering in a murder investigation, and so would
any judge. And this is once too often. I'm being fair. I
have apologized for accusing you of something I can't
prove. But by God, I can prove this."

Wolfe put his palms on the chair arms. "Mr.

Cramer. I know, of course, what you're after. You have no intention or desire to charge me formally with obstructing justice; that would be both troublesome and futile. What you want is to learn whether I got any information that would help you in a case that has you baffled; and if I did, you want to know what it is. I'm willing to oblige you, and to the full. As you know, Mr. Goodwin has an extraordinary memory. Archie. Give Mr. Cramer our conversation with Miss Porter last evening. In toto. Omit nothing."

I shut my eyes for a moment to concentrate. Getting it straight with no fumbling would be a little tricky, with all the names and titles and dates, and the way Wolfe had steered it along to the main point. Evidently, for some reason, he wanted Cramer to have it all, and I didn't want him stopping me to insert something I was leaving out. I started slow, speeded up when I got going, and tripped only once, when I said "extortion" instead of "attempted extortion," and I caught that and corrected it. Toward the end, knowing that I had it by the tail, I leaned back and crossed my legs just to show that there was really nothing to it for a man of my caliber. Finishing, I yawned. "Sorry," I said, "but I'm a little short on sleep. Did I skip anything?"

"No," Wolfe said. "Satisfactory." His eyes went to Cramer. "So you have it, every word. There was manifestly no attempt to interfere with a homicide investigation; murder was mentioned only incidentally. You are welcome to the information I got from her."

"Yeah." Cramer didn't sound grateful. "I could put it under a fingernail. She didn't tell you a single solitary thing. And I don't believe it, and you don't expect me to. Why did you let her *go?* You had her. You had her backed into a corner that she couldn't possibly squirm out of, and you quit and sent her home. Why?"

Wolfe turned a hand over. "Because nothing more was to be expected of her, at the moment. She had identified X for me. More accurately, she had given me a hint, a strong one, and I wanted to confirm it. I have done so. Now that I know him, or her, the rest should be easy."

Cramer took a cigar from his pocket, stuck it in his mouth, and clamped his teeth on it. I wasn't as impressed as he was, since the second I had seen Wolfe lean back and shut his eyes and start his lips going I had known there would soon be some fireworks, though I hadn't expected anything quite so showy. Not caring to have Cramer know that this development was as new to me as to him, I yawned again.

Cramer removed the cigar. "You mean that, do you? You know who killed Simon Jacobs and Jane Ogilvy and Kenneth Rennert?"

Wolfe shook his head. "I haven't said so. I know who wrote those stories and instigated the plagiarism claims. You're investigating a series of murders; I'm investigating a series of frauds. I have my X and you have yours. True, the two Xs are the same person, but I need only expose a swindler; it will be your job to expose a murderer."

"You know who he is?"

"Yes."

"And you got it from what Alice Porter told you last night? And Goodwin has repeated all of it?"

"Yes. I have confirmed the hint she gave me."

Cramer's fingers had closed on the cigar, which was probably no longer fit for chewing, let alone smoking. "Okay. That's not your kind of lie. What was the hint?"

"You have heard it." Wolfe's fingertips met at the peak of his middle mound. "No, Mr. Cramer. Surely that's enough. I asked Mr. Goodwin to repeat that conversation, and I told you it contained a disclosure of the identity of X, only because I felt I owed you something and I don't like to be in debt. I know what it cost you to tender me an apology. Even though you did it in desperation, because you're stumped, and even though you immediately reverted to your customary manner, it took great will power and I appreciate it. So now we're even. You know everything that I know, and it will be interesting to see whether you get your murderer first, or I my swindler."

Cramer stuck the cigar in his mouth, learned too late that it was in shreds, jerked it out and threw it at my wastebasket, and missed by two feet.

A while back, when it took me nearly two hours to spot the screw Wolfe was going to use on Alice Porter, I remarked that you had probably seen it and thought me as dumb as they come, and now of course you are thinking that Cramer and I were both dumb, since you have almost certainly caught on to the hint Wolfe had got from Alice Porter and you now know who X was. But you're reading it, and Cramer and I were in it. If you don't believe that makes a big difference, try it once. Anyhow, even though you now know X's name, you may be curious to see how Wolfe nailed him—or her. So I'll go on.

When Cramer left, some ten minutes later, he wasn't curious because there wasn't room enough in him for it. He was too damn sore. When I stepped back into the office after going to the hall to see that he didn't forget to cross the sill before he shut the door, the phone was ringing and I went and got it. It was

Saul Panzer. He asked for Wolfe, and Wolfe, lifting his receiver, told me, "You might catch Miss Ballard before she goes to lunch."

I may not be much at hints, but I got that one. I departed.

Chapter 18

Of all the thousands of ways of getting a credit mark from a woman, young or old, high on the list is to take her to lunch at Rusterman's, the restaurant that was owned and operated by Marko Vukcic when he died. Since Wolfe is still the trustee of the estate, there is always a table for me, and when Cora Ballard and I edged through the crowd to the green rope and Felix caught sight of me, he led us to the banquette at the left wall. As we sat and took our napkins Cora Ballard said, "If you're trying to impress me you're doing fine."

I'm all for Wolfe's rule not to discuss business at meals, but that time it couldn't be helped because she had to be back at her office by two-thirty for an appointment. So after we had taken a sip of our cocktails I said I supposed she knew a good deal about all of the NAAD members. No, she said, not all of them. Many of them lived in other parts of the country, and of those in the metropolitan area some were active in NAAD affairs and some weren't. How well did she know Alice Porter? Fairly well; she had always come to craft meetings until recently, and in 1954, when Best and Green had decided to publish her book, *The*

Moth That Ate Peanuts, she had visited the NAAD office several times for advice on the contract.

Time out to get started on our ham timbales.

What I was after, I said, was a document that we had reason to believe Alice Porter had left in some-body's care. Did members deposit important documents with the NAAD for safe-keeping? No, the association had no facilities for that kind of service. Did she have any idea with whom or where Alice Porter might leave something very important—for instance, an envelope to be opened if and when she died?

She had started a loaded fork to her mouth but stopped it. "I see," she said. "That might be pretty smart, if— What's in the envelope?"

"I don't know. I don't even know there is one. Detectives spend most of their time looking for things that don't exist. Mr. Wolfe thought it was possible she had left it with you."

"She didn't. If we started doing things like that for members we'd have to have a vault. But I might have some ideas. Let's see. . . . Alice Porter." She opened her mouth for the forkload.

She had six ideas:

1. Alice Porter's safe-deposit box. If she had one.

2. Mr. Arnold Green of Best and Green, who had published her book. He was one of the few publishers who liked to do favors for authors, even one whose book had been a flop.

3. Her father and mother, who lived somewhere on the West Coast, Miss Ballard thought in Oregon.

4. Her agent, if she still had one. Lyle Bascomb had taken her on after her book had been published, but he might have dropped her by now.

5. The woman who ran Collander House on West 82nd Street, the hive-home for girls and women who

couldn't afford anything fancy, where Alice Porter had lived for several years. Her name was Garvin, Mrs. Something Garvin. One of the girls in the NAAD office was living there now. She was the kind of woman anybody would trust with anything.

6. The lawyer who handled her suit against Ellen Sturdevant. Cora Ballard couldn't remember his name, but I did, from the pile of paper I had waded through at the office.

Over the years I have chased a lot of wild geese, but that was about the wildest, asking a bunch of strangers about something that maybe didn't exist, and if it did maybe they had never heard of it, and if one of them had it why should he tell me? So I spent five hours at it. I tackled Lyle Bascomb, the agent, first, because his office was only a short walk from Rusterman's. He was out to lunch and would be back any minute. So I waited fifty minutes. He returned from lunch at 3:33, and his eyes were having a little trouble focusing. He had to think a minute before he could remember who Alice Porter was. Oh yes, that one. He had taken her on when she had a book published, but had dropped her when she made that plagiarism claim. I gathered from his tone that anyone who made a plagiarism claim was a louse.

At the lawyer's office I had to wait only thirty minutes, which was an improvement. He would be glad to help. When a lawyer says he will be glad to help he means that he will be glad to relieve you of any information you may have that he could ever possibly use, and at the same time will carefully refrain from burdening you with any information that you don't already have. That one wasn't even going to admit that he had ever heard of a woman named Alice Porter until I told him I had read three letters signed by him

referring to her as his client. I finally pried it out of
him that he hadn't seen her or communicated with her
for some time. Two years? Three? He couldn't say defi-
nitely, but an extended period. As for the information
he relieved me of, I will only say that I put him under
no obligation.

It was after five o'clock when I arrived at the office
of Best and Green, so it was a tossup whether I would
catch him, but I did. The receptionist halted a lipstick
operation long enough to tell me that Mr. Green was in
conference, and I was asking her if she had any idea
how long the conference would last, when a man appeared from within and headed for the door, and she
called to him, "Mr. Green, someone to see you," and I
went for him, pronouncing my name, and he said, "I'm
making a train," and loped out. So, as I say, I caught
him.

I had used up half of Cora Ballard's ideas. Of those
left, two weren't very promising. There are about a
thousand banks with safe-deposit vaults in New York,
and anyway I didn't have keys to all the boxes, and
besides, it was after hours. Taking a plane to the West
Coast to look up Alice Porter's parents seemed a little
headlong. Finding an empty taxi in midtown Manhattan at that time of day was almost as hopeless, but I
finally grabbed one and gave the driver the address on
West 82nd Street.

Collander House could have been worse. The girl in
the neat little office had a vase of daisies on her desk,
and the room across the hall, which she called the
lounge, where she sent me to wait for Mrs. Garvin, had
two vases of daisies, comfortable chairs, and rugs on
the floor. Another thirty-minute wait. When Mrs. Garvin finally appeared, one straight look from her sharp
gray eyes confirmed Cora Ballard's statement that

anyone would trust her with anything. Certainly she remembered Alice Porter, who had lived there from August 1951 until May 1956. She had the dates in her head because she had looked them up at the request of a city detective last week, and had recalled them that morning because a woman had come and asked about Alice Porter. She hadn't seen Alice Porter for three years and was keeping nothing for her. Not even some little thing like an envelope? No. Which didn't mean a thing. She was a busy woman, and it was quicker to say no than to explain that it was none of my business and have me trying to persuade her that it was. A lie isn't a lie if it is in reply to a question that the questioner has no right to ask.

All in all, a hell of an afternoon. Not one little crumb. And the immediate future was as bleak as the immediate past: another meatless dinner for Wolfe, after a beerless day. More gloom. He would be there at his desk, glaring into space, wallowing in it. As I climbed out of the taxi in front of the old brownstone I had a notion to go to Bert's diner around the corner and eat hamburgers and slaw and discuss the world situation for an hour or so, but, deciding it wouldn't be fair to deprive him of an audience, I mounted the stoop and used my key on the door; and, with one foot inside and one out, stopped and stared. Wolfe was emerging from the kitchen, carrying a large tray loaded with glasses. He turned in at the office. I brought my other foot in, shut the door, and proceeded.

I stood and looked it over. One of the yellow chairs was at the end of my desk. Six of them were in two rows facing Wolfe's desk. Five more of them were grouped over by the big globe. The table at the far wall was covered with a yellow cloth, and on it was an assortment of bottles. Wolfe was there, transferring the glasses from the tray to the table.

I spoke. "Can I help?"

"No. It's done."

"A big party, apparently."

"Yes. At nine o'clock."

"Have the guests all been invited?"

"Yes."

"Am I invited?"

"I was wondering where you were."

"Working. I found no envelope. Is Fritz disabled?"

"No. He is grilling a steak."

"The hell he is. Then the party's a celebration?"

"No. I am anticipating events by a few hours. I have a job ahead of me that I prefer not to tackle on an empty stomach."

"Do I get some of the steak?"

"Yes. There are two."

"Then I'll go up and comb my hair."

I went.

Chapter 19

Wolfe, at his desk, put down his coffee cup and sent his eyes to the ex-chairman of the Joint Committee on Plagiarism. "I like my way better, Mr. Harvey," he said curtly. "You may ask questions when I finish if I haven't already answered them." His head went right, and left. "I could merely name the culprit and tell you that I have enough evidence to convict her, but while that would complete my job it wouldn't satisfy your curiosity."

Mortimer Oshin had the red leather chair ex officio. The committee members and the executive secretary had the six yellow chairs in front of Wolfe's desk. In the front row were Amy Wynn, nearest me, then Philip Harvey, and then Cora Ballard. In the rear were Reuben Imhof, Thomas Dexter, and Gerald Knapp—the three publishers. Grouped over by the big globe were Dol Bonner, Sally Corbett, Saul Panzer, Fred Durkin, and Orrie Cather. In a spot by herself, at the end of my desk, was Alice Porter, who was sipping root beer from a glass that was perfectly steady in her hand. I had coffee. The others had their choices—gin and tonic, scotch and soda, scotch and water, rye and ginger ale, bourbon on the rocks, and one, Oshin, cognac. Evidently Oshin knew brandy. After he had taken a sip he had asked if he might see the bottle and had studied the label thoroughly, and after another sip he had asked, "For God's sake, how much of this have you got?" I had taken the hint and given him a dividend, and he hadn't lit a cigarette for at least five minutes.

Wolfe's head went right and left again. "I should explain," he told them, "the reason for Miss Porter's outburst. It was justified. She is here because I lied to her. I told her on the phone that I was prepared to hand her a paper signed by Mr. Imhof and Miss Wynn in exchange for one signed by her. The word 'prepared' was a misrepresentation. When this discussion is ended I am confident that Miss Porter will be in no fear of prosecution by Mr. Imhof or Miss Wynn, but I was not actually 'prepared' when I phoned her this afternoon. In fairness to her I must say that her indignation, when she arrived and found a crowd, was warranted. She stayed because I told her I was going to demonstrate to you that she was guilty of a criminal act and I advised her to hear me."

Alice Porter blurted, "You just admitted you're a liar!"

Wolfe ignored it. "I'll give you the essentials first," he told the committee, "and the conclusions I reached, and then fill in the details. A week ago yesterday, eight days ago, Mr. Goodwin gave you a full report of the brief talks he had had with those four people— Simon Jacobs, Kenneth Rennert, Jane Ogilvy, and Alice Porter. I don't know if any of you noticed that his talk with Miss Porter was quite remarkable—that is, her part of it. He told her that a New York newspaper was considering making her a substantial offer for the first serial rights to her story, and what did she say? That she would think it over. Beyond that, not a word. Not a question. All seven of you know writers better than I do, but I know a little of men and women. Miss Porter was not a famous and successful author; her only book had been a failure; her stories were barely sufficient, in quantity and quality, to preserve her standing as a professional. But she didn't ask Mr. Goodwin the name of the newspaper. She asked him nothing. I thought that remarkable. Did none of you?"

"I did," Cora Ballard said. "But she was on a spot. I thought she was just scared."

"Of what? If she doubted Mr. Goodwin's bona fides, if she suspected that he might not have such an offer from a newspaper, why didn't she question him? At the very least, why didn't she ask him the name of the newspaper? It seemed to me a fair surmise that she didn't doubt or suspect Mr. Goodwin; she *knew* he was lying. She knew that this committee had hired me, and that he was trying by subterfuge to get a copy of the story on which she had based her claim against Miss Wynn. At the moment—"

"How could she know?" Harvey demanded. "Who told her?"

Wolfe nodded. "Of course that was the point. At the moment the surmise was only of minor interest, but the next day, when it was learned that Simon Jacobs had been murdered, it took on weight; and more weight when Jane Ogilvy too was killed; and still more when Kenneth Rennert made it three—and Alice Porter was still alive. Attention was focused on her, but I continued to doubt that she was the target because I could not believe that she had invented a style of com-

position for 'There Is Only Love' for her claim against
Ellen Sturdevant, and imitated it for 'What's Mine Is
Yours' for the claim made by Simon Jacobs against
Richard Echols, and again imitated it for 'On Earth
but Not in Heaven' for the claim made by Jane Ogilvy
against Marjorie Lippin, and then abandoned it and
used her natural style for 'Opportunity Knocks' for the
claim made by her against Amy Wynn. But last evening—"

Mortimer Oshin cut in, "Wait a minute. What if she
knew how that would look?" There was still a little
cognac in his glass, and he still hadn't lit a cigarette.

"Just so, Mr. Oshin. Last evening Mr. Goodwin
brought her here, and after an hour with her I asked
that question myself. What if she had been shrewd
enough to realize in advance, at the time she enlisted
Simon Jacobs in the plot against Richard Echols, that
the best shield against suspicion would be a modus
operandi so fantastic that she would not even be considered? After an hour with her I thought it possible
that such superlative cunning was not beyond her; at
least it was worth exploring. When she had gone I
spent an hour on the telephone, getting five people,
highly competent detectives who help me on occasion;
and when they came at eight o'clock this morning I
gave them assignments. They are present and I wish
to introduce them. If you will please turn your heads?"

They twisted around.

"In front at the left," Wolfe told them, "is Miss Theodolinda Bonner. Beside her is Miss Sally Corbett. In
the rear at the left is Mr. Saul Panzer, next to him is
Mr. Fred Durkin, and at the right is Mr. Orrie Cather.
I should explain that before they went on their sepa-
rate errands they were supplied with photographs of

Alice Porter, procured by Mr. Panzer at a newspaper office. I'm going to ask them to report to you. Mr. Cather?"

Orrie got up and went to the corner of Wolfe's desk and stood facing the committee. "My job," he said, "was to find out if she had ever been in contact with Simon Jacobs. Of course the best place to start was with the widow. I went to the apartment on Twenty-first Street and there was no one there. I asked around among the other tenants, and I—"

"Briefly, Orrie. Just the meat."

"Yes, sir. I finally found her at a friend's house in New Jersey. She didn't want to talk, and I had a time with her. I showed her the photograph, and she recognized it. She had seen the subject twice about three years ago. The subject had come to the apartment to see her husband and had stayed quite a while both times, two hours or more. She didn't know what they had talked about. Her husband had told her it was about some stories for a magazine. I tried to get her more exact on the time, but the closest she could come was that it was in the spring of nineteen fifty-six and the two visits were about three weeks apart. Her husband hadn't told her the name of the subject."

Wolfe asked, "Was her recognition of the photograph at all doubtful?"

"No, she was positive. She recognized it right away. She said she—"

Alice Porter blurted, "You're a liar! I never went to see Simon Jacobs! I never saw him anywhere!"

"You'll get a turn, Miss Porter," Wolfe told her. "As long a turn as you want. That will do, Orrie. Miss Corbett?"

Sally Corbett was one of the two women who, a couple of years back, had made me feel that there might be some flaw in my attitude toward female dicks. The other one was Dol Bonner. Their physical characteristics, including their faces, were quite different, but were both of a description that makes a woman looked at from a personal viewpoint; and they were good operatives. Sally went and took Orrie's place at the corner of Wolfe's desk, turned her head to look at him, got a nod, and faced the audience.

"My job was the same as Mr. Cather's," she said, "except that it was with Jane Ogilvy instead of Simon Jacobs. I didn't get to see Mrs. Ogilvy, Jane's mother, until this afternoon. I showed her the photograph and asked her if she had ever seen the subject. After studying it she said she was pretty sure she had. She said that one day more than two years ago the subject had come to see her daughter, and they had gone to the cloister. If you have read the newspapers you know about the building that Jane called the cloister. In half an hour or so they returned to the house because the electric heater in the cloister was out of order. They went up to Jane's room and were there for three hours or more. Mrs. Ogilvy didn't learn the subject's name and never saw her again. By association with other matters she figured that it was in February, nineteen fifty-seven that the subject had come to see her daughter. She didn't make the identification positive, but she said she could, one way or the other, if she saw the subject in person instead of a photograph."

I turned my head for a look at Alice Porter. She was on the edge of the chair, rigid, her eyes half closed, her head thrust forward, and her lips parted with the tip of her tongue showing. She was looking at Wolfe, oblivious of the eight pairs of eyes, including

mine, that were aimed at her. When Sally Corbett returned to her chair and Fred Durkin took her place at
the corner of Wolfe's desk, Alice Porter's gaze didn't
leave Wolfe, even when Fred spoke.

"I had Kenneth Rennert," Fred said, "and the trouble was there wasn't any widow or mother or anyone
like that. I saw about twenty people, other tenants in
the building and the building superintendent, and
friends and acquaintances, but none of them recognized the subject from the photograph. From two or
three of them I got a steer to a restaurant on Fifty-
second Street, the Pot-au-Feu, where Rennert often
ate lunch and sometimes dinner, and that was the only
place I got anything at all. One of the waiters, the one
that had the table where Rennert usually sat, thought
the subject had been there twice with Rennert, once
for lunch and once for dinner. He was cagey. Of course
he knew Rennert had been murdered. He might have
opened up more if I had slipped him a twenty, but of
course that was out. He thought it had been in the late
winter or spring last year. He thought if he saw the
subject he could tell better than from a photograph.
He had liked Rennert. The only reason he talked at all
was because I told him it might help to get the murderer. I think if he was sure of that and if he saw the
subject in person—"

Wolfe stopped him. "That will serve, Fred. The ifs
are ahead of us. Mr. Panzer?" As Fred went back to
his chair and Saul came forward, Wolfe told the committee, "I should explain that Mr. Panzer's assignment
was of a different nature. It was given to him because
it required illegal entry to a private dwelling. Yes,
Saul?"

The committee had Saul's profile because he was
turned to face Alice Porter. "Yesterday evening," he

said, "as instructed, I drove to Alice Porter's home near Carmel, arriving at twelve minutes past ten. I opened the door with a key, one of an assortment I had, and entered, and made a search. On a shelf in a cupboard I found some sheets of paper with typewriting, clipped together, twenty-five pages. The first page was headed 'Opportunity Knocks,' and below that it said 'By Alice Porter.' It was an original, not a carbon. I have delivered it to Mr. Wolfe."

He glanced at Wolfe, and Wolfe spoke. "It's here in a drawer of my desk. I have read it. In plot and characters and action it is identical with the story, 'Opportunity Knocks,' by Alice Porter, the manuscript of which was found in a file in the office of the Victory Press. But that one, the one found in the file, was written in Alice Porter's natural style, the style of her published book, *The Moth That Ate Peanuts*, whereas this one, the one found by Mr. Panzer in Miss Porter's house, was written in her assumed style, the one she had used for the three stories on which the previous claims had been based. Call them A and B. The obvious inference is that in writing the story that was to be the basis for her claim against Amy Wynn she had tried both styles, A and B, and had decided, for whatever reason, to use the one in style B. What else did you find, Saul?"

Saul's eyes were again on Alice Porter. "That was all in the house," he said. "But she had gone to New York with Mr. Goodwin in his car, so her car was there, and I searched it. Under the front seat, wrapped in newspaper, I found a knife, a kitchen knife with a black handle. Its blade is seven inches long and an inch wide. I have delivered it to Mr. Wolfe. If he has examined it with—"

He sprang forward. Alice Porter had bounced out of her chair and dived for Amy Wynn, her arms stretched and her fingers curved to claws. I was right there, so I had her right arm half a second before Saul got her left one, but she had moved so fast that the fingernails of her left hand got to Amy Wynn's face before we jerked her back. Philip Harvey, on Amy Wynn's right, had lunged forward to intervene, and Reuben Imhof, back of Amy Wynn, was on his feet, bending over her. Alice Porter was trying to wriggle loose, but Saul and I had her back against Wolfe's desk, and she gave it up and started yapping. She glared at Amy Wynn and yapped, "You dirty sneak, you double-crosser, you dirty sneak, you double—"

"Turn her around," Wolfe snapped. Saul and I obeyed. He eyed her. "Are you demented?" he demanded.

No answer. She was panting. "Why assault Miss Wynn?" he demanded. "She didn't corner you. I did."

She spoke. "I'm not cornered. Tell them to let go of me."

"Will you control yourself?"

"Yes."

Saul and I let go but stayed between her and Amy Wynn, and Harvey and Imhof were there too. She moved back to her chair, and sat. She looked at Wolfe. "I don't know if you're in it with her," she said, "but if you are you'll regret it. She's a liar and a murderer and now she thinks she can frame me for it, but she can't. Neither can you. That's all lies about my seeing those people. I never saw any of them. And if that story was found in my house and that knife was found in my car she put them there. Or you did."

"Are you saying that Amy Wynn killed Simon Jacobs and Jane Ogilvy and Kenneth Rennert?"

"I am. I wish to God I had never seen her. She's a liar and a sneak and a double-crosser and a murderer, and I can prove it."

"How?"

"Don't worry, I can prove it. I've got the typewriter that she used to write that story, 'There Is Only Love,' when she got me to make that claim against Ellen Sturdevant. And I know how she planted it in a bureau drawer in Ellen Sturdevant's house. And that's all I'm going to tell you. And if you're in it with her you're going to regret it." She stood up, bumping me. "You get out of my way." Saul and I stayed put.

Wolfe's tone sharpened. "I'm not in it with her, Miss Porter. On the contrary, I'm in it with you, up to a point. I ask one question, and there's no reason why you shouldn't answer it. Did you write an account of your association with Miss Wynn, put it in an envelope, and entrust the envelope to someone with instructions that it was to be opened if and when you died?"

She stared. She sat down. "How did you know that?"

"I didn't. I surmised it. It was the simplest and best way to account for your remaining alive and not in trepidation. Where is it? You might as well tell me, now that its contents are no longer a secret. You have just revealed them, their essence. Where is it?"

"A woman named Garvin has it. Mrs. Ruth Garvin."

"Very well." Wolfe leaned back and took a breath. "It would have made things easier for both of us if you had been candid with me last evening. It would have saved me the trouble of all this hocus-pocus to force you to speak up. Miss Wynn did not put a manuscript in your house or a knife in your car. Mr. Panzer did not go there last evening. He spent the day composing and typing the kind of story he described because I thought you might demand to see it. He also bought the kind of knife he described."

Alice Porter was staring again. "Then that was all lies. Then you *were* in it."

Wolfe shook his head. "If by 'in it' you mean a conspiracy with Miss Wynn to make you pay for her crimes, no. If you mean a trap to force the truth out of you, yes. As for Mr. Cather and Miss Corbett and Mr. Durkin, they told no lies; they merely permitted you to infer that the photographs they showed to various people were of you, but they weren't. They were photographs of Amy Wynn—and by the way, we can now hear from Miss Bonner. You needn't leave your chair, Miss Bonner. Report briefly."

Dol Bonner cleared her throat. "I showed a photograph of Amy Wynn to the woman who runs Collander House on West Eighty-second Street, Mrs. Ruth Garvin. She said that Amy Wynn lived there for three months in the winter of nineteen fifty-four and fifty-five, and that Alice Porter also lived there at that time. Is that enough?"

"For the present, yes." Wolfe's eyes moved to take in his client, the committee. "That, I think, should suffice. I have established a link between Miss Wynn and each of her four accomplices. You have heard Miss Porter. If you wish, I can proceed to collect ample evidence to persuade a jury to convict Miss Wynn of her swindles, but it would be a waste of your money and my time, since she will go to trial not for extortion, but for murder, and that is not your concern. The police and the District Attorney will attend to that. As for—"

Reuben Imhof suddenly exploded. "I can't believe it!" he cried. "By God, I *can't* believe it!" He appealed to Amy Wynn. "For God's sake, Amy! Say something! Don't just sit there! Say something!"

I was back in my chair, and by stretching an arm I could have touched her. She hadn't moved a muscle since Wolfe had asked Alice Porter about the envelope. Her hands were pressed flat against her breasts, as if to hold them up, and her shoulders were pulled back, far back. Down her right cheek, from just below the eye almost to her jaw, were two red streaks where Alice Porter's nails had scraped. She paid no attention to Imhof and probably she didn't hear him. Her eyes were fixed on Wolfe. Her lips moved but there was no sound. Someone muttered something. Mortimer Oshin took his empty glass from the stand, went to the table at the far wall, poured a triple portion of brandy, took a swallow, and came back.

Amy Wynn spoke to Wolfe, her voice so low that it was just audible. "You knew that first day," she said. "The first time we came. Didn't you?"

Wolfe shook his head. "No, madam. I had no inkling. I am not clairvoyant."

"When did you know?" She might have been in a trance.

"Last evening. Alice Porter gave me the hint, unwittingly. When I showed her that her position was untenable and told her that I would advise you to prosecute, she was not concerned, she said you wouldn't dare, but when I added that I would also advise Mr. Imhof to prosecute she took alarm. That was highly suggestive. Upon consideration I sent her home, and I did something I might have done much sooner if there had been the faintest reason to suspect you. I read your book, *Knock at My Door,* or enough of it to conclude that you had written the stories on which the first three claims had been based. That was manifest from the characteristics of your style."

Her head moved, slowly, from side to side. "No," she said. "You knew before that. You knew the third time we were here. You said it was possible it was one of us."

"That was only talk. At that point anything was possible."

"I was sure you knew," she insisted. "I was sure you had read my book. That was what I'd been afraid of since the second time we came, when you told us about comparing the stories. That was when I realized how stupid I had been not to write them in a different style, but you see I didn't really know I had a style. I thought only good writers had a style. But I was stupid. That was my big mistake. Wasn't it?"

They were all staring at her, and no wonder. From her tone and her expression you might have thought Wolfe was conducting a class in the technique of writing and she was anxious to learn. "I doubt if it could properly be called a mistake," he said. "A little thoughtless, perhaps. After all, no one had ever compared the stories before I did, and I wouldn't have compared them with your book if I hadn't got that hint from Miss Porter. Indeed, Miss Wynn, I wouldn't say that you made any mistakes at all."

"Of course I did." She was quietly indignant. "You're just being polite. All my life I've been making mistakes. The biggest one was when I decided I was going to be a writer, but of course I was young then. You don't mind if I talk about it? I want to."

"Go ahead. But fourteen people are listening."

"It's you I want to talk to. I've been wanting to ever since the first time we came and I thought you knew. If I had talked to you then I wouldn't have had to—to do what I did. But I didn't think you would say I didn't make any mistakes. I shouldn't have told Alice about you. You told us when you started, I mean when you started today, that she gave it away that she knew about our hiring you when Mr. Goodwin told her he had an offer from a newspaper, and so your attention was focused on her. But I had made the worst mistake with her before that, when she claimed my book was plagiarized from a story she wrote. Of course I know that was poetic justice. I know I deserved it. But after so many years, when I actually had a book published, and the first printing sold out, and then three more printings, and it was actually third on the best-seller list, and then my publisher got that letter from Alice, I lost my head. That was an awful mistake. I should have told her I wouldn't pay her anything, not a cent. I should have dared her to try to make me. But I was so scared I gave in to her. Wasn't that a mistake?"

Wolfe grunted. "If so, not an egregious one. She had the upper hand—especially after the manuscript of her story was found in a file in your publisher's office."

"But that was part of the mistake, my putting it there. She made me. She said if I didn't she would tell everything—about the claim against Ellen Sturdevant, and of course that would bring it out about the others. And she told me—"

"My God." Reuben Imhof groaned. He had gripped her arm. "Amy, look at me. Damn it, look at me! *You* put that manuscript in that file?"

"You're hurting my arm," she said.

"Look at me! You did that?"

"I'm talking to Mr. Wolfe."

"Incredible." He groaned again. He let go of her arm. "Absolutely incredible."

Wolfe asked, "You were saying, Miss Wynn?"

"I was saying that she told me about what she had put in an envelope and left with somebody to be opened if she died. I don't see how you can say I didn't make any mistakes. I hadn't realized how dangerous it was for her to have the typewriter I used to write that story for her to use, 'There Is Only Love.' We thought it would be a good idea for her to have it because she was supposed to have written the story, but I hadn't realized that it could be traced to me because I had bought it. I had bought it secondhand, but typewriters have numbers on them somewhere. You can't say I didn't make any mistakes. You ought to say I didn't do anything right. Did I?"

"If by 'right' you mean 'well,' you did indeed."

"What? What did I do well? Tell me."

"It would take an hour, Miss Wynn. You did a thousand things well. Your conception and execution of the swindles were impeccable, providing for all details and avoiding all pitfalls. Your choice of accomplices was admirable. Your handling of the situation these past two weeks has been superb. I have had some experience with people under stress wearing masks, both men and women, and I have never seen finer performances than yours—the first time you called on me with your fellow committee members, two weeks ago today, when I questioned you at some length; the second time, when Mr. Oshin made his suggestion about Simon Jacobs and asked you to contribute ten thousand dollars; later that day at Mr. Imhof's office when Mr. Goodwin was told of the discovery of the manuscript which you had yourself put in the file; the third time you came with the committee, when the question whether to dismiss me was debated; the meeting of that council yesterday, when that question was again discussed in my presence—your performance on all of those occasions was extraordinary."

Wolfe turned a palm up. "On one occasion you showed ready and notable wit—on Friday, four days ago, when Miss Porter drove to New York to see you at your apartment. By then, of course, she was confronting you with a direr menace than exposure of your swindles; she was threatening to reveal you as a murderer. That is true?"

"Yes. That's why she came to see me. How did I show any wit?"

Wolfe shook his head. "Mr. Imhof used the right word for you, Miss Wynn. 'Incredible.' Apparently you have performed prodigies of sagacity and finesse without knowing it. Not surely by inadvertence; it must be that your singular faculties operate below the level of consciousness—or above it. Perhaps the psychologists should add a new term, superconscious. When Miss Porter came to your apartment on Friday afternoon did she tell you that she had been followed?"

"No. But I was afraid that maybe she had been."

"That makes it even better. Brilliant. So you telephoned Mr. Imhof and told him Miss Porter was there with an offer to settle her claim, and asked his advice. You don't call that brilliant?"

"Of course not." She meant it. "It was just common sense."

Wolfe shook his head again. "You are beyond me. Added to your other achievements, you committed three murders in an emergency with such resourcefulness and dexterity that a highly skilled police force is completely at sea. I offer a suggestion. I suggest that you request the District Attorney to arrange for your brain to be turned over to competent scientists. I shall myself suggest it to Mr. Cramer of the police. Will you do that?"

A sound came from Cora Ballard, half gasp and half moan. It was the first sound from any of them except Imhof since Dol Bonner had reported. No one looked at her. No one was looking at anyone but Amy Wynn.

"You're just being polite," Amy Wynn said. "If I had any brains this wouldn't be happening. It's crazy to say I didn't make any mistakes."

"You made one," Wolfe said. "Only one of any consequence. You shouldn't have allowed the committee to hire me. I don't know how you could have managed it, but I don't know how you have managed any of your miracles, and you don't either. If it had occurred to you, you would have done it somehow. I am not crowing; I merely say that it is unlikely that anyone else would have hit upon the combination of maneuvers by which you have been exposed. You wanted to talk. Have you anything else to say?"

Her nose twitched. "You have never shaken hands with me."

"I rarely shake hands with anyone. I beg you not to offer yours."

"Oh, I wouldn't expect you to now." She stood up. "No, there's nothing else. I had some things to do before I—I have some things to do." She was moving.

She *was* incredible. I was absolutely glued to my chair. I don't say that if there had been only the three of us, Wolfe and her and me, I would have sat there and let her walk out, but the fact remains that I didn't stir. She passed, in no hurry, in front of Philip Harvey and between Cora Ballard and Mortimer Oshin; and when, four paces from the door, she found her way blocked by Saul and Fred and Orrie, she turned square around and looked at Wolfe. Just looked. No more talk. Her nose twitched.

Wolfe turned his head to me. "Get Mr. Cramer, Archie."

Another sound came from Cora Ballard, louder than before, as I swiveled to get the phone.

The World of
Rex Stout

Now, for the first time ever, enjoy a peek into the life of Nero Wolfe's creator, Rex Stout, courtesy of the Stout Estate. Pulled from Rex Stout's own archives, here are rarely seen, never-before-published memorabilia. Each title in "The Rex Stout Library" will offer an exclusive look into the life of the man who gave Nero Wolfe life.

Plot It Yourself

Here is a letter to Rex Stout from his longtime editor at the Viking Press, Marshall Best, after the galleys of *Plot It Yourself* had been legally vetted. (Neither Callas nor Best ever sued). The book—written in a remarkable thirty-four days during the early summer of 1959—was published by Viking in October. The original dust jacket is reproduced here.

THE VIKING PRESS INC · PUBLISHERS
625 MADISON AVENUE · NEW YORK 22 · NY
Cable: Vikpress   Telephone: PL 5-4330

July 31, 1959

Mr. Rex Stout
High Meadow
Brewster, N. Y.

Dear Rex:

Jim Grossman has had his fun with PLOT IT
YOURSELF and the only character he worries about
for libel is Maria Callas. Shall we let her sue?

Unless you want to worry about Best and Green. . .

I am sending you an extra set of galleys for
your own use. If you don't want them, you know
what you can do with them.

Sincerely,

Marshall

MAB:nb

PLOT IT YOURSELF

a Nero Wolfe novel

REX STOUT

REX STOUT'S NERO WOLFE

A grand master of the form, Rex Stout is one of America's greatest mystery writers. Now, in this ongoing program dedicated to making available the complete set of Nero Wolfe mysteries, these special collector's editions will feature new introductions by today's best writers and never-before-published memorabilia from the life of Rex Stout.